Praise for C

'**A small miracle** – sharp
Ni

'Part comic romp and part nail-biting thriller... Castle Freeman writes with **both wit and a deep understanding of the human psyche**, and he does not cheat us out of a dramatic climax.' *Guardian*

'Shares many small-town, big-crime themes with Cormac McCarthy... it is **impossible not to appreciate this**.' *The Times*

'**Wonderful... every paragraph a gem**. Freeman – like Cormac McCarthy, like Annie Proulx – shows us the awkward realness of lives, and does it with humour, with wry perception, with great style.' R. J. Ellory

'Extremely funny... streamlined storytelling, dead-on dialogue and lyrical descriptions of the bleak, woodsy landscape. This is a **meticulous New England miniature, with not a word wasted.**' *Oprah Magazine*

'A fast, memorable read gooey with atmosphere ... **a gem that sparkles with sly insight and cuts like a knife.**' *Boston Globe*

'Freeman has a flawless ear for dialogue and a sharp eye for quirky detail ... **Superb**.' *People Magazine*

'A brilliant book – **laconic, spare, stylish and exciting**.' Al Alvarez

'**A small masterpiece of black comedy and suspense** ... If all novels were this good, Americans would read more.' *Kirkus Reviews*

OLD NUMBER FIVE

Castle Freeman

Have you read them all?

Treat yourself again to the Lucian Wing novels by
Castle Freeman –

All That I Have

A local tearaway gets tangled up with big-league criminals on
Sheriff Wing's patch

Old Number Five

Lucian Wing ends up drawing on his last ounces of patience,
tact, and – especially – humour.

Children of the Valley

A pair of runaways take refuge in Sheriff Wing's slice of the
Vermont countryside.

Turn to the end of this book for a full list of Castle
Freeman's books, plus – on the last page – the chance
to receive **further background material**.

THE FIFTH COMMANDMENT
Honour thy father and thy mother:
that thy days may be long upon the land
which the Lord thy God giveth thee.
—King James Bible: *Exodus* 20:12

Contents

1	The New Arrangement	11
2	Sprinters	20
3	The Bell	27
4	D F K	34
5	Everything in Families	45
6	The Elephants' Graveyard	51
7	The Look-See	58
8	Calamity Jane	64
9	The Iron in Her	75
10	The Soft Path	82
11	A Grapefruit Spoon	87
12	The Intimidator and the Infield	93
13	Steep Mountain Follies	100
14	The Situation	107
15	Old Number Five	115
16	The Click	123
17	The Deal-Breaker and the Pass	130
18	The Tree Stand	137
19	Death of the Don	148
20	Recohabitation Day	155
21	The Orchard	162
22	Sherlock F. Holmes	167
23	New Information	175
Envoi		184

1

The New Arrangement

One time, our mother told me a thing. 'You know?' she said, 'everybody always thinks the brains in this family is your brother. Wrong. It's you. You're a lot smarter than Paul. No, you are. But your trouble is, you're lazy. Paul ain't lazy.'

If she had been talking to Paul instead of me, she would have said *isn't*. And if you can get hold of that, if you can understand it, if you can enjoy it, then you may like this story. If not, well, in that case, you might do best to take your business to another shop.

That's what Clemmie had done, it looked like: taken her business to another shop. Or taken the shop to the business, you could say. I didn't know. I did know Clemmie and her new-old friend Jake were spending a good deal of time together, had been for six, eight weeks. I knew Jake was in and out of Clemmie's and my new place on Diamond Mountain a lot. A lot more than I was. Had Jake moved in with Clemmie? Was my place his place, now? I didn't know that either, but I meant to find out. I meant to find out.

In any case, somebody was doing business, all right, and it wasn't me. While Clemmie and Jake carried on in our house, the house we'd built together, I'd been living in the office on Sheriff

Ripley Wingate's, my old boss's, gut-sprung couch, which, when the weather was damp, still smelled like Wingate's five-for-a-buck cigars. In there, I had a coffee machine, an electric ring and a pot for cooking. I had the couch and a sleeping bag. I listened to the radio, and when I couldn't sleep I went out front and played chequers with the Prince of Darkness – that being what we called Walt, the night dispatch. Nickel a game.

Yes, at the time I'm telling of, there we were, in a whole new arrangement: Clemmie and Jake sawing my wood at what had been my home and now looked like being theirs, and I camped out in my office in Fayetteville, doing my job.

About that job. It ain't a job just like everybody else's job. It ain't a normal job. I'm the county sheriff up here in our valley. I enjoy my work. Our valley is a pretty valley. It's a good valley. It's a quiet valley, mostly. People think I go along doing nothing. But there's doing nothing, and then there's doing nothing – and doing it right. Everyplace needs the second, from time to time, even if it comes to no more than a little push on one side or the other, a drop of oil in season. The sheriff can give the push. The sheriff holds the oil can.

Then there's another thing about our valley. It's a pretty valley, it's a good valley, and the rest. But it ain't a large valley. That means, for the sheriff and everybody else, we're swimming in the same puddle, like tadpoles in a spring pool. The more we dart around, the more we run into ourselves. Therefore, arrangements like this new one Clemmie and Jake and I seemed to have made can get a little awkward from time to time. They can get to be like trying to play touch football in a phone booth. There are new rules, there have to be. What are they?

'Lucian, now. Lucian?' Jake said. 'We always got along. I ain't looking for any trouble with you. You know how things sometimes work out.'

Jake was coming out of the store with a case of beer and a package of frozen shrimp.

'Things?' I asked him.

'Uh, things. You know.'

'Clemmie won't eat that,' I told Jake. 'She don't like shrimp.'

'It's for the cat,' Jake said.

'The beer, too?'

'Huh?'

'Is the beer for the cat, too?'

'Uh, no,' Jake said. 'The beer's for me.'

'Nothing for the little woman?'

'Huh?'

'What's for Clemmie? Mrs. Wing? My wife? What's she going to eat?'

'Uh, I don't know,' Jake said. 'Something. I guess.'

'I guess so,' I said. 'Hell of a cook, ain't she?'

'Huh?'

'Clemmie's a good cook, ain't she?'

'Oh,' Jake said. 'Oh, yeah, she is.'

'Okay, Jake,' I said. 'We'll see you.'

'I'm glad there's no hard feelings.'

''Course not,' I said.

'I hate that fucking cat, you know it?' Jake said.

That was Jake. That was Clemmie's new business. 'She'll be back,' said Mom. 'Clemmie Jessup hasn't got a brain in her head, never has had. And now she's hooked up with Jake Stout? I don't know whether to laugh or cry. He's dumber than she is. Wire the two of them's brains together and turn the switch, they wouldn't light up a Christmas tree bulb. When Clemmie figures that out, she'll be back. I told you, she's got no brains at all.'

Our mother set Hell's own store by brains.

ıt are you saying, exactly?' I asked her. 'If Clemmie's so
ıat does that make me?'

'Smarter than Paul,' Mom said.

***

I was helping my old friend Gus Cooper point a chimney in
West Galilee. I do a good deal of that kind of thing, working
around, more than you might think. I work around because I
have to. In olden days (I'm talking about Merry England and
so on) the sheriff of a county was a rich and powerful man.
He went to work in a fancy coach with footmen and outriders
tooting horns. No more. Today the sheriff's office is for hire
to provide law enforcement to country towns too small, too
poor (they say) to have their own police force. The selectmen in
those towns do not like to spend money. They slice the bacon
pretty thin. They want to be safe and secure, but they don't
see why the sheriff and his deputies should need to eat more
than once a day or put wood in the stove in winter. The town
fathers are tightly budgeted, they'll tell you, and they mean
that you should be, too. No coach and four, no footmen. The
Sheriff of Nottingham, I ain't. Therefore I pick up a little side
income from one local contractor or another helping on jobs:
masonry, stonework, painting, building, roofing, and the like.
Banging nails and carrying things from here to there. Nothing
too ambitious. No plumbing. No electric.

'Your boss just drove up,' Gus said. He was on the roof peak,
at the chimney. I was down in the yard at the ladder's foot,
seeing to the mix and waiting for Gus to need fresh. I couldn't
see the driveway, but Gus could.

'Who?' I asked him.

'You know. The Chairman.'

'He ain't my boss,' I said.

14

'He's everybody's boss, I thought.'

'Tell him I'm not here?'

'Your rig's here,' Gus said. He was waving to somebody.

'All right,' I said. 'You coming down?'

'Hell, no,' Gus said. 'I'm good where I am. He's all yours.'

'Thanks,' I said.

'Don't be too long,' Gus said. 'You're on the clock, you know.'

I went around the house and found Stephen Roark waiting for me beside his vehicle. He was not happy.

'You're a hard man to reach, aren't you, Sheriff?' Roark said.

Stephen Roark was the chairman of the board of selectmen in Cardiff, my own town, the third-largest town in the county. We're lucky to have Stephen. Just ask him; he'll tell you the same thing. He had done us the favour of arriving in our community only a couple of years earlier, on his retirement from the United States Air Force. He was Colonel Roark, as a matter of fact, and he had the habits of his rank about him: the habit of command, the habit of intimidation, the arrogance – all that, though Roark had had his career in an office at the Pentagon and had never heard a shot fired in anger. As Wingate, a combat veteran of the Second World War, said of Roark, there is no man a harder, stronger, more iron-bound soldier than a peacetime colonel.

'You're a hard man to reach,' Roark said. 'Don't you have a phone?'

'Good morning, Mr. Roark,' I said.

I called Stephen Mister Roark. I didn't call him what most people did, which was Chairman Steve, or the Chairman. That name was meant to zing. On the town board, Roark made a big point of being the Chairman, of the board of select*men*. He would have no part of titles that got around the question of male and a female: no chairperson, no select board, no select people, and so on. Unfortunately for him, Roark's conviction put him right up against Sally Anthony, the longest-serving member of the board and a lady every bit as tough, every bit as self-righteous as Roark, and very nearly as obnoxious. Sally lost no chance to refer to Roark as the Chairman. 'What's the Chairman's position?' 'Shall we ask the Chairman?' 'Point of order, please, Mister Chairman?' Many others in town, including Gus Cooper, were glad to stick it to Roark a little by calling him the Chairman as Sally did, or Chairman Steve, or simply The Chair. Not me, though. If you're the sheriff, you know sooner or later you're going to get everybody in the district pissed off at you for one reason or another. No need to go out looking for the piss.

'Don't you have a phone?' Roark was asking me.

'Course I have a phone,' I said.

'Well, doesn't it work? I've been trying to get you all morning. If you've got a phone, where is it?'

'In my truck.'

'What the hell good is it in the truck if you're not? You're up on the roof, or wherever. The phone's in the truck. You can't hear it.'

'Why it's in the truck.'

Roark gave me a look that was as though I was putting out a powerful odour. He took a breath. He shook his head. 'Do you know what happened at the clinic last night?' he asked.

'I heard some kid came in.'

'Terry St. Clair,' Roark said. 'He didn't come in. I brought him in. I found him in the road. He was semiconscious. He could have bled to death. His hand was gone.'

'Gone?'

'Cut off,' Roark said. 'He'd lost a lot of blood. He almost didn't make it. It just happened I was driving home. I know the kid. He's done work for me.'

'I know him, too,' I said. 'I know him well. Terry's in and out of trouble like it's McDonald's. What did he say happened?'

'He didn't,' Roark said. 'He was passed out. At the clinic they were trying to keep him alive. I left. I called this morning. He's there. He'll be okay. Except for the hand.'

'I'll go see him,' I said.

'I'll go with you,' Roark said.

'No need.'

'I'm going with you, Sheriff,' Roark said. 'I'm a town official. The victim is known to me. I'm concerned. I'm very concerned. Do you get that? I'm going.'

'Suit yourself,' I said.

So I punched out on Gus, who was not happy, but was used to my unreliable ways, and I drove to the clinic followed by Roark. The Chairman. I'd call him the Chairman. Sure, I would. I was ready to call him whatever he wanted. I'd call him God Almighty if it would make him happy. He wasn't happy. He was concerned, he was very concerned. And Stephen Roark, the Chairman, by whatever name, if he was concerned, very concerned, was bad news for me.

At the clinic, they had Terry St. Clair flat on his back in bed and hooked up to two IV bags, one for blood and another that ought to have held a dose of brains but was probably mostly water. Terry looked like hell. He was a kind of grey-blue-white colour, and the bandaged stump of his left arm, down to about three inches above the wrist, was hung up on a chain above his chest. He was awake, but he wasn't talking. With me and others in my line of work, that wasn't unusual for Terry, even at his best. Terry was what you might call an amateur, part-time petty criminal. In the city, he would have made his way easily enough, but up here he had to struggle, he had to take on honest work from time to time – for example, odd jobs around Chairman Roark's big place in North Cardiff. But if Terry didn't come up to the highest standard of criminality, still he knew the rules. He wasn't interested in talking to the Law.

'They treating you okay?' I asked Terry.

'I guess,' he said.

'Are you in pain?'

'I guess.'

'Have they been giving you anything for the pain?'

'I guess.'

Roark stepped in. He didn't exactly push me aside, but he might as well have.

'What happened to your hand, Son?' he asked Terry.

Terry looked at me. He had been looking at Roark while I questioned him, but now he turned his head to look at me. He didn't answer.

'Son?'

'I was baling,' Terry said. 'It was the baler.'

'You were baling hay?' Roark asked Terry.

Terry nodded.

'In the middle of the night?'

Terry looked at me again. A long look. 'That's right,' he said.

'Come on,' Roark said.

'Fuck you,' Terry said. 'I said all I'm going to say.'

The door of the room opened, and the doctor or resident, or whatever you're to call who's on duty at a place like the clinic, came in.

'Sheriff,' he said, 'you're going to have to cut this short. He's in no shape. You can see he isn't.'

The medic, Roark and I left Terry and went out into the corridor.

'He had a very near thing,' the medic said. 'He was in shock. He had minutes when he came in. Not a lot of minutes, either. Did you bring him?' he asked me.

'I did,' Roark said.

'You saved his life, then,' the medic said. 'Simple as that.'

'What did that to his arm?' Roark asked him. Who was running this investigation, anyway? It looked like the Chairman was. Let him have it, then, right? 'He says he got caught in a baler,' Roark kept after the medic. 'Could a baler have taken off his hand like that?'

'I don't know,' the medic said. 'Why ask me? I'm not a mechanic. I'm a taxidermist. I'm not a farmer. I don't know balers. I doubt it like fury, though.'

'What, then?'

'Well,' the medic said, 'that was one stroke. Cut clean. So, something heavy. Something heavy. Something sharp.' He shrugged.

'You mean, like an axe?' Roark asked him.

'Maybe,' said the medic. 'Or, more like, a big knife or a cleaver. Like a butcher's cleaver?'

'Can I see him later?' I asked.

'Up to him,' the medic said. He left us. Roark took off then, too, and I started back to Gus's job. I thought I'd come to the clinic on my own and have a word with Terry, maybe the next day. Though, really, for what? We weren't going to get any more out of Terry. Being short a hand was part of Terry's trouble, it was a big part, but it was only part. Mainly, Terry was scared. He was scared of something – and it wasn't Chairman Roark. And it wasn't me.

I didn't blame him. If I'd been Terry, I'd have been scared, too.

2

Sprinters

The next afternoon, or it might have been the day after that, I had a call at the sheriff's office from Addison Jessup, Clemmie's dad, my father-in-law. 'Come on out, later,' Addison said.

'I can come now,' I told him. 'What is it?'

'No, come after you close up shop,' Addison said. 'We'll have a drink. Any time after five.'

Any time after nine a.m., you mean, is what I thought but did not say. This was a fellow who liked his toddy.

Addison swung a fairly heavy bat in our valley. He lived in the big old house in South Devon where Clemmie had grown up. Addison and Monica, Clemmie's mother, had split up when she was little. Her mom had been a New Yorker. She moved back to the city, remarried, and pretty much dropped off Clemmie's screen: expensive birthday and Christmas presents; vacation trips; younger step-brothers and –sisters. And that was it. She pretty much left parenthood to Addison.

Addison had stayed put. He was an attorney, though he never seemed to work too hard at it. He didn't scramble around going to real estate closings and writing wills and drawing up nickel-and-dime trust instruments. Not Addison. He didn't spend a lot of time in court. He was in the advice business, as he put it, rather than the straight-on law business; and most of the people he advised were out of town. You could say Addison was a corporation lawyer – or he would have been, if we'd had any corporations in the valley. Now he was taking it easy, in permanent semi-retirement, enjoying the Golden Years among his books and his empties.

I found him on the screen porch in back. On the table beside him, a bucket of ice and a family-size bottle of Johnny Walker's. I always thought Addison should move to Scotland. A man should be close to the thing he loves.

'Lucian,' Addison said. 'You're looking well. Sit down. Let me pour you one.'

'Maybe later,' I said. I sat.

'Come off it,' Addison said. 'Join me. It's five-thirty. You're not on duty any longer, are you?'

'You tell me what you want, and I'll tell you if I'm on duty.'

'Had a call from Clemmie.'

'I thought so,' I said. 'Keep your liquor.'

Addison and I always got along very well. Why wouldn't we? I was the fellow who took Clemmie off her father's hands at last – Clemmie, as a daughter, like Clemmie, as a wife, being, in her own sweet way, a piece of work. Now, when Clemmie didn't want to talk to me, she used her old man as a kind of ambassador. That was what this visit was for, I thought; Clemmie wanted something. So I told Addison to save his liquor.

'Steady, Lucian,' Addison said. 'Take a breath. Count to fifty. You know our girl: you've got to give her time. She'll come across.'

'Come across?' I said. 'She's already coming across, ain't she? Ask young Jake Stout if she ain't. I can't go into my own house at night for fear I'll trip over the two of them.'

'I'm not defending her,' Addison said. 'I'm not denying Jake is a peculiar choice on her part.'

21

'I don't care about her and Jake. They can do what they want, where they want. It's just I'm getting sick of living on the couch, there.'

'You can always stay here. Plenty of room.'

'Hah,' I said. 'You better look out. I might take you up on that.'

'Any time,' Addison said.

'You said she called. What does she want?' I asked him.

Addison took from his pocket a note and a pair of half-glasses that he settled on the end of his nose. He read. 'Let's see,' he said. 'Pane came out of the kitchen window, broke, needs new glass. Hot faucet on the kitchen sink drips. Bulb over the back door is out.' He passed the note to me and took off his glasses. 'God damn it,' he said, 'I don't know why her friend Jake can't put in a new light bulb. I'm going to tell her so, by god.'

'Don't do it,' I said. 'I wouldn't trust Jake with the job. I built that house with my own two hands. I sawed every two-by-four. I hammered every nail. I'm damned if I'll let a moron like Jake work on the place.'

'You and Clemmie built it, you mean,' Addison said.

'You're right,' I said. 'She helped. We did it together. If she wants to fix stuff, that's fine. But she won't. She won't lift a finger. She has to call you to call me.'

'That's my little girl,' Addison said 'You know why she does that, don't you?'

'I know why you think she does it.'

'Sure, you do,' Addison said. 'She does it to keep you in play. Clemmie's a cautious investor, don't you know. That's what she is. She likes having her assets out in the markets working, going up, going down – but she also likes having some in the bank, where they're safe.'

'Her assets?'

Addison chuckled. 'Be patient,' he said. 'She'll be back.'

'Meantime, what about me? I'm a handyman in my own home. I don't get paid. I don't even get laid.'

'Relax. It's not forever. You'll see. She'll come around.'

'That's what Mom said.'

'Your mother is a shrewd woman. I've always said so. A shrewd, shrewd woman.'

'Maybe she is,' I said. 'It don't change that I'm being made a fool of.'

'Not at all,' Addison said. 'Nobody thinks any the less of you. Believe me, they don't. On the contrary. You're making friends, Lucian, more than you know. All the world loves a cuckold.'

'Is that a fact?'

'You ready for a drink, now?'

'Just a short one,' I said.

Addison fixed the drinks and handed me a glass. I began to take a sip when Addison went on.

'Saw a friend of yours yesterday,' he said.

I paused. 'Who was that?' I asked him.

'Steve Roark. The selectman.'

I put my glass, untasted, down on the table.

'The Chairman?' I said. 'The Chairman's no friend of mine.'

'I'd have to agree,' Addison said.

'How's it you know him?'

'State bar association. Roark and I were talking after the last meeting.'

'Bar association? The Chairman's a lawyer, too?'

'We're everywhere, Lucian.'

'I thought he was a military man,' I said.

'He is,' Addison said. 'Was. Judge Advocate's office. He's a member of the DC bar, so he's in up here, too. Reciprocity. Too bad. The man's an unmitigated shit. He thinks he's General

Patton. Nobody can stand him. Doesn't matter. Never misses a meeting. Last one, your name came up.'

'How?'

'Something about somebody's arm that got cut off?'

'Hand,' I said. 'That's right.'

'Roark was talking about that. He knows the young fellow. He thinks he was assaulted.'

'He thinks something, don't make it so.'

'He wasn't entirely satisfied with your response as sheriff, I gathered.'

'What's he want? It's an open case. We're working on it.'

'Of course, you are. I told him that. I defended you. But Roark's learned there have been other similar incidents since he's been in town.'

'One or two,' I said.

'Somebody else, he said, lost an ear. I think I remember that, don't I? Buddy Carpenter? Chainsaw kicked back on him. Couple of years ago.'

'That's right.'

'Then there was the time young Lewis got hurt.'

'That's right.'

'What's become of Lewis?'

'Left town, I think.'

'Yes,' Addison said. 'And what about the Bancroft boy? Sam? Scott? Shot himself in the foot that time?'

'Tommy. It seems like he's left town, too.'

'Quite a string, then,' Addison said.

'I don't know,' I said. 'Over a few years? I don't know about a string. Accidents happen. And, plus, it's not like anybody's sorry those boys are gone, is it?'

'True,' Addison said. 'They were bad news, to a man. Good riddance, I agree. But the Chairman mentioned them. And then he wanted to know about you. How long you've been sheriff. What your background in law enforcement is. What the sheriff's duties are. How he's elected. When. What kind of oversight he gets. Things of that nature.'

'Does he know we're, uh, related?' I asked Addison.

'I told him we were. I told him you knew your job.'

'He didn't believe you.'

'That was my impression, too,' Addison said. 'No friend, as you say. Don't let him get you down, Lucian. What's he going to do, impeach you?'

'I never heard of anybody impeaching the sheriff.'

'Of course you haven't. Ignore him. I only mention it because I thought you'd want to know. About Roark's interest.'

'I appreciate it,' I said.

'Stephen Roark's a sprinter, Lucian,' Addison said. 'You know that. He's a classic sprinter. Sprinters come, they're here, they go. Wait him out.'

'Wait him out,' I said. 'You've got me doing quite a lot of waiting, here, don't you? I'm waiting on Clemmie. Now I'm waiting on the Chairman. It looks as though all I'm doing is waiting.'

'You and everybody else,' Addison said.

***

A sprinter, Addison said. Chairman Steve's a sprinter. Sprinter was our name for a certain kind of newcomer you get in the little country towns up here. This fellow relocates from the city. He follows the moving van into town, arrives on Monday. Tuesday, he unpacks. Wednesday, he shows up at the regular meeting of the town's board of selectmen. Friday, he's a member of the board. The next Tuesday, he's the board's chairman. Another week, and he's a justice of the peace and serving as a lister. If our towns had mayors, that would be the sprinter's next move, but they don't; he's gone as far as he can go at home, so he has to elevate his sights. He runs for the state legislature. Nobody else wants the job, so he wins. Now he's in Montpelier mostly. Locally, he begins to go down, so to speak, he begins to drain off, like muddy water after a flash flood. Suddenly, he's scarce. Pretty soon, he's out of sight.

While the sprinter is among us, we get the benefit of his fresh perspective, of his experience in the larger world. We get the benefit of all that he knows, and we get the benefit of all that he don't know. As for example, the Chairman and Terry St. Clair's business. The thing is, Roark really has no idea where he is. He thinks he's still at the Pentagon, with the bigshots. Wrong. We're not bigshots up here. We're working people. We're working with heavy equipment. We're working in the woods, in the quarries, on the roads, on the farms. It's hard work. It ain't like working for the Judge Apricot or whoever he is. We get tired. Then we get hurt. Like I told Addison: accidents happen. The Chairman don't understand that. He never will. And I don't have time to teach him, even if he were teachable, which he ain't.

Well, then, if you've got somebody that you can't teach, you can't give him orders, and you can't shut him up – what do you do with him?

3
The Bell

It was the weekend before I got out to our place with Clemmie's punch list. Could I have made it sooner? Sure, I could. I aimed to stand Clemmie up a little. Let her wait. Clemmie don't like to wait. But, the way I see it, I'm married to Clemmie; I ain't her employee. I ain't her servant. Sometimes she needs to be reminded of those things. Sometimes she needs to hear the bell.

When I drove up, she was out in front, on her hands and knees, looking under the front porch of our house. Jake's truck was parked to one side of the house, beside Clemmie's Accord. Was he here? Maybe I'd find out, though I didn't expect he'd show himself. Jake was a little shy of me lately, I'd noticed. I couldn't imagine why.

Clemmie got to her feet and came toward me. She didn't look happy, and I thought she was going to light into me for not getting there before today, but no.

'It's Stu,' she said. 'He's missing. He never came in last night. I thought he might have gone under the porch again.'

Stu was our cat. He was a fat, fluffy black-and-white thing that looked like an overgrown skunk. Stu was Clemmie's cat mainly, but he was polite to me. He would have nothing to do with Jake. I liked Stu.

'Don't worry about him,' I told Clemmie. 'He's okay. He's taken off before.'

'I know he has,' Clemmie said. 'But, the thing is, Jake's been hearing coyotes at night, the last couple of nights. Help me look for him, okay?'

'Jake's been hearing coyotes? At night? You surprise me. I'd thought he'd be sound asleep, all the exercise he gets in here.'

'So funny,' Clemmie said.

'Where is my friend Jake, anyway?' I asked her. 'I don't see him. I'd hate to have missed him.'

'Um, he's at work,' Clemmie said.

'What's his truck doing here, then?'

'He got a ride,' Clemmie said. 'Are you going to help me look for Stu, or aren't you?'

'What for? If he's hiding out in the woods, we'll never find him. He'll come in or he won't. Probably he won't. It's not real healthy out there, you know, for Stu. Jake hears coyotes. Or, wait. Maybe Stu ran into the Don.'

'I don't believe that nonsense about the Don,' Clemmie said, 'and neither do you.'

'Sure, I do,' I said. 'Why not? Point is, either way, you won't find Stu. If coyotes got him, if the Don got him, you won't want to.'

'So, no, you won't help look,' Clemmie said.

'I'll help,' I said.

We went around the house, through the yard, looking here and there, calling Stu's name, and then we went on into the woods behind. Our little lot ends at the brook in back. From the brook the land goes up Diamond Mountain in heavy woods right to the ridge. There are no houses up there, no roads except some old logging tracks. It's steep, brushy, hard going. That's where the coyotes live, along with other things. Looking for a lost cat in those woods, or for any other lost thing that's smaller than a battleship, is pretty much a waste of time. After half an hour Clemmie understood that. We gave it up and went back down to the house. There, I got my tools from the truck and started toward the house to do the fixing Clemmie had told her dad about, but,

'Do that another time, okay?' Clemmie asked.

'Another time?' I said. 'You're the one wanted this done. You're the one said I was to come. Here I am.'

'That was four days ago,' Clemmie said. 'You didn't make it then. Now it's not convenient.'

'Not convenient?'

'Not convenient.'

Ding, went the bell.

'Why not?' I asked Clemmie.

'It just isn't.'

I set my toolbox carefully down on the tailgate of the truck. 'I'm sorry to hear that,' I said to Clemmie. 'I'm sorry you're inconvenienced. That's tough. Especially since you generally have things pretty convenient, on the whole, don't you? Wouldn't you say?'

Clemmie didn't answer. She crossed her arms over her chest and sent me a look that might have been used in the kitchen to kill ants.

'I'd say so,' I answered myself. I was getting warmed up now. 'Pretty convenient, things are, for you, I'd say. You're out here, nice house, rent-free, debt-free, got the cable, got the cat, your new used Accord. Got the invisible, on-demand, all-weather boyfriend. You've even got free maintenance. That's me. I'm the maintenance man. But sometimes I don't get right to it, do I? Sometimes I run late. Know why?'

Now Clemmie was looking serenely up at the blue sky. The passing clouds, the sunlight, the little birds flying by had all her attention.

'Bad back,' I said. 'Mornings, my back hurts. Can barely move, some mornings. I think maybe it's from sleeping on that old couch. The one in my office. That one. You know, it ain't the most comfortable bed, that couch. Some people would call it inconvenient.'

'Are you enjoying this?' Clemmie asked me. 'Are you having fun? Please, tell me.'

'Not really, no,' I said. 'I am not having fun. That's because, like you, I hate inconvenience. I hate it. And I am finding it wicked inconvenient living on a couch in my office.'

'Where else have you ever?'

'Say what?' Clemmie can shift gears as quick, as smooth, as they can do it at Indianapolis or Daytona. You have to see it to believe it.

'Where else have you ever lived?' she was asking me now. 'You were living in your office when we first got together – or you might as well have been. You've been living in your office ever since, too, the whole time we've been married. Your body might have been here with me – rarely – but you weren't. Not ever. You were in your office. On your couch.'

'Now, look,' I began, but,

'On your fucking couch,' Clemmie said. She's up near full r.p.m.s now; you can tell by her mouth. 'Or,' she went on, 'or, you were galloping hither and yon minding everybody else's business and being a legend in the valley. Who knew a little valley like this one even needed a legend? Who knew it could have so many places for a legend to go so he wouldn't have to be home?'

'Now, look.'

'*You* look,' Clemmie said. 'If I'd known I was marrying a legend, I'd have stayed single. Being married to a legend is no picnic, you know? Really, it isn't. It's lonely, for one thing. It's lonely, and it's boring.'

'Boring?'

'Boring,' Clemmie said. 'Now, if you'll excuse me?'

Ding. End of the round.

'I'll come back for this stuff,' I said, meaning the window pane, the faucet, and so on. 'Or, I can do them now.'

'I told you,' Clemmie said. 'Not today.'

'I don't care if he's here,' I said.

'Lord, Lucian: *he's not here,*' Clemmie turned and went back toward the house.

I climbed into the truck and got ready to back around to the road when I happened to glance at the house, just in time to see the curtains in the upstairs bedroom window part, then close again. Somebody had been peeking out from behind the curtain, watching us. Jake? Clemmie had said he was at work, but it didn't look that way, did it? I'd wondered if Jake had moved in, hadn't I? Well, maybe his hiding in the bedroom didn't make it for sure, but it didn't say no, either. Nothing did.

Driving away, I looked to one side of the road and the other into the woods for some sign of Stu the cat. Nothing there, of course. I didn't hold out much hope for poor Stu. That mountain was full of wildlife that would love to make a meal of him: not only coyotes, but foxes, fishers, owls – not counting the giant killer dog that was supposed to live in those woods. Clemmie didn't think he was there, but I wasn't so sure. Wingate had seen him. So had others. His name was Don Corleone.

This was an Italian mastiff, a fighting dog, bred not to hunt but to go into a little cage or a pit with another dog like it and close and bite and grip and rip until one or both of them had bled to death. A brindle dog, according to Wingate, heavy headed, heavy shouldered, and big – had to have weighed 150. It had belonged to a half-crazy pensioned-off New York City police officer named Calabrese, a near-hermit who had had a trailer on the other side of Diamond Mountain. Calabrese had planned to breed these dogs; this one was to be the stud, if that's what you call it in the dog business. Too bad for Calabrese, though, before he got everything set up, he dropped dead of a heart attack one day while feeding the dog. (At least that's what looked to have happened when we went over the place.) The pen's gate wasn't secure, the dog got out and took off. Ever since, it had been running wild. All up and down the valley, it took sheep, pigs, even cattle. Calabrese had named the dog Don Corleone, after another Italian who was a nice enough fellow in his way but would just as soon kill you as not. If Stu had gotten into Don Corleone's sights? Well, as Calabrese himself would have said: forget about it.

***

Boring, Clemmie said. Among other things, she said, living with me is boring. I expect it is, too. Steady, reliable, patient, honest, are what I am. Women are supposed to like that, I thought, ain't they? Some of them? Clemmie used to. She said so. With her mother completely out of the picture, and her father busy being a leading citizen in what time he could find between drinks, Clemmie was looking for a solid, permanent fellow she could put in the bank and know he was there, the way Addison said. She got that. She liked it for a while. Now she's bored. But not for long. Jake will see to that, when he comes out from behind the curtain. Or, how about this? Maybe Jake was at work like Clemmie said, and somebody else was up in the bedroom. Our bedroom. My bedroom. Why not? Any number can play. Just as long as Clemmie ain't bored.

Addison once told me, he said, 'Lucian, you and Clemmie have an Open Marriage, that's what it is. We had one, too, Monica and I, for a while, but we didn't call it that. We called it fooling around, or we called it cheating, or sometimes we called it adultery. Now it's an Open Marriage. It's not unusual these days. Everybody's got one. Enjoy it. You've got your end, too, you know? Cut loose.'

He was right, I guess, but as for my end, I don't think so. The thing is, Clemmie and I don't have just any old Open Marriage. We have an Open Marriage of a special kind. It's open for Clemmie, but it ain't open for me. It looks like our Open Marriage is closed at one end, like a cracker box or a minnow trap.

Well, after all, it's what happens when a lady marries beneath herself, ain't it? It wasn't for nothing that our mother called Clemmie The Infanta; and that's what Clemmie did: she married beneath herself. Don't believe me? Ask anybody. Ask Clemmie.

4
D F K

Wingate said he wasn't surprised. 'You take a fellow like that,' he said, 'a fellow who's so successful, so sure of himself? He gets to be a certain way. What you have to remember: he ain't really in his right mind. I saw it in the war, over and over. The top guys, the brass? All nuts, every man-jack. 'Course, they weren't all of them nuts in the same way. They were different. Some of them thought it was part of God's plan for them to get what they wanted, in everything, every time. Some thought, no, that wasn't them; they didn't need God. They were just naturally a thousand percent smarter, stronger, tougher, better, more qualified, more deserving than anybody else, and so of course they were on top. They couldn't understand that what they had and where they'd gotten to was mainly because of luck, just like it is with the rest of us.'

We had been talking about the Chairman. His taking an interest in Terry St. Clair's trouble. His putting the spurs to me. His raising hot and general hell. Wingate wasn't surprised, he said.

'I don't know,' I told Wingate. 'I ain't one of Chairman Steve's biggest fans, but I don't think he's crazy.'

'As a loon,' Wingate said. 'remember, you heard it here first. But, look: I'm giving you the benefit of my superior age and experience, that's all. Take what you want. You think Mr. Roark is sane and sound, go ahead and think that. But don't sell him short, and don't think he'll go away. He won't. Any normal person, a thing like Terry's thing, in time he'd just let it slide. Not Roark. That's what I mean.'

'I know it,' I said.

We were at Wingate's, sitting out back on his camp chairs. Wingate was smoking a cigar. He gave himself three cigars a day, and he smoked them outdoors. In winter he smoked on the little side porch out of the snow; rest of the time he smoked in the yard. Wingate's wife had been gone for a number of years, but when she was alive she had a strict no-smoking policy for inside the house; and now Wingate kept her rule. He said if he didn't Gracie would probably come back to haunt him, and although he said he'd like that in a way, he reckoned it would be easier without.

'I don't know,' Wingate was saying. 'With fellows like Roark? Today? Your job? It's a harder job than it was in my day.'

'You're damned straight right, it is.'

'No,' Wingate said, 'I mean it. It is. My day, people would mainly let you do your job the way you thought best. They didn't try to check up on everything and supervise all the time. They trusted you. If they didn't, they'd vote for somebody else next time, and away you'd go. Today, everybody's the sheriff. Roark, the other selectmen, the town clerk, everybody. I suppose it's on account of the giant salary you're getting now.'

'That must be it.'

'How's Clementine?' Wingate asked. I'd been waiting for this.

'She's great,' I said.

'I'm glad to hear it. Didn't somebody or other tell me you two haven't been getting along?'

'It's a lie. Since she kicked me out of the house, we've been getting along fine.'

'Kicked you out? Where did you go?'

'Office. I'm based in the office, temporarily.'

'You mean our office? The old office? Not a lot of room there.'

'No.'

'Again, it's the job,' Wingate said. 'This work, being sheriff, any kind of peace officer, I guess, is hard on a marriage.'

'Yours did okay. How long were you married?'

'Fifty-two years,' Wingate said. 'But that's because I married a schoolteacher. Gracie was always a lot more interested in her kids than she ever was in me. Me, she pretty much ignored. So I kind of snuck in over behind, you might say. Listen, you want to come here? You can have the spare room.'

'I'm okay where I am. Thanks, though. Addison offered the same thing. Everybody in town wants to put me up.'

'You're a popular young fellow, it looks like, don't it?'

Wingate's a clever old guy, but he's wrong about Chairman Roark. Wingate thinks he's nuts. Chairman Steve ain't nuts. His trouble is, he takes things too seriously. He works too hard. He's a driver, and that may be okay in the Air Force, where he came up, but it don't work around here. These little towns, their people, they'll get to where they have to go, but they can't be driven. They have to be let to get there on their own. Things take care of themselves, not always in a way that's perfect, or neat, or gentle, or just even. Not in a way that makes everybody happy, or anybody happy. But things work themselves out, if they're allowed to. That's what the Chairman don't understand. He'll drive and prod and crack the whip, but it won't work. He won't get what he wants. And if he keeps on like he's going, he'll get what he don't want.

'Terry's going to be okay, ain't he?' Wingate asked.

'Well, he's going to live. Course, losing a hand ain't nothing.'

'Which hand?'

'Left hand.'

'Yes, that's tough,' Wingate said. 'Terry being a southpaw.'

'That hand being his stealing hand,' I said.

'It's a disablement, all right,' Wingate said. 'It's a reminder.'

'Pretty rough stuff for a reminder.'

'Reminder's your word, way I recall,' I said.

'So it is,' Wingate said. 'Sometimes a reminder has to be rough. Sometimes nothing else works.'

'I know,' I said.

'I know you know,' Wingate said.

***

Wingate knew I knew because it was he who had let me know. Truth is, I haven't always been the law-abiding, law-upholding, law-enforcing model citizen you see before you. As a misbehaving youth, I was right up there with the worst – or down there, I guess I mean. Twenty years ago, three or four of my pals and I were the curse of the valley. We ran on alcohol, gasoline, and what-do-you-call-it – testosterone – and we ran as hard as we could. We burned privies, we chased and if possible caught and rode horses, cows, sheep, and other livestock, we painted the Bethany post office black, we broke a thousand windows, we let the air out of a thousand tires, we put a thousand cherry bombs in a thousand rural letter boxes. When one of us, Chipper Ness, got sent to the state school, where he learned to hotwire cars, we stepped our game up to taking other people's vehicles – once including one of Sheriff Wingate's cruisers – for fast rides. Fast and expensive.

Sure, we settled down eventually. Some of us got smart: Gus Cooper does very well with his masonry contracting business; and Danny Tucker is an engineer with the state highway department. Some of us settled down because we hadn't much choice: Chipper is doing federal time in Tennessee. As for me, I was persuaded to sign for a stretch in the Navy, came home, put in a couple of years as a state police trooper, and then joined the sheriff's department. When Wingate offered to take me on as his deputy, he told me he was doing it because he knew from past experience with me that the two of us would be working together a good deal, one way or another, and having us working mostly on the same side seemed to him to make sense.

I don't know, even today, if what I have in the sheriff's office is a career. I never planned for it to be one. But if it is, if a life in this work is what I'm going to have, then it's because of Wingate. It's because I got picked up, turned around, and my feet set down, pretty firmly, on the right, straight path, by Wingate. Or anyway with his help. In fact, there were three of them: Wingate; Homer Patch, the town constable in Gilead; and Cola Hitchcock – Old Cola, this was, of course, the father of the Cola of today, who has the junkyard in Dead River Settlement.

They called it a reminder. The three of them stopped me late at night on the road to Mount Nebo. I thought Wingate was busting me for driving drunk, which I was not (that night); though I couldn't make out what Homer and Old Cola were doing riding with him.

'Am I under arrest, here?' I asked.

'Hell, no, you ain't,' Cola said. 'We're going to a party. You like parties.'

'I don't think I want to go to this one, though,' I said.

'You got to,' Homer said. 'You're the guest of honour.'

Wingate didn't speak.

They put me in Wingate's truck with Cola. Wingate drove. He was in his own vehicle, not a sheriff's cruiser. Homer followed us in my car. We drove up Mount Nebo to where the road ended, far back in the woods. Old Cola had a hunting camp in there, his father had had it before him. All that land in Mount Nebo is state land now, as it was then, but Cola's family had what they called an in-holding, or some such, a kind of special deed that let them own and use their camp and a couple of acres around it. The Hitchcock men (mostly, it was men) and their family and friends stayed up there in season and hunted deer, bear, wild turkeys, and the rest.

What Cola's place was was for-real, sure-enough, old-fashioned Vermont deer camp. You could have stuffed it and put it in a museum. In fact, it already was a museum. It was a museum of itself.

You left your vehicle on an old log landing and walked in to the camp, a quarter of a mile. The camp building was framed of rough two-by-fours and sheathed in bare black tarpaper; no siding. It was one room fifteen feet square fitted with bunk beds along two walls, dusty, never-washed windows, a dry sink, a central table, eight or ten chairs, some hard, some soft, and a big oil-drum stove that burned wood. The walls inside were vertical pine boards covered with newspapers turned yellow with age. You could read about the attack on Pearl Harbor on the walls of Cola's camp; you could read about DiMaggio and Harry S Truman. Above the sink were shelves for canned goods, bottles of one thing and another, generally things having a certain alcohol content, and the poker chips and cards.

Outside, the tarpaper walls were decorated with nailed-up antlers and turkey wings. There was no electric, no running water. Cola's camp operated on the basis of kerosene lanterns, water toted from the brook in buckets, and a privy back behind.

We sat around the table. The three men looked at me, looked at one another. Nobody seemed to know where to begin. At last Wingate spoke. He asked me, 'Like boats, do you, young fellow?'

'Boats?' I said. 'You mean like rowboats? Canoes?'

'No,' Homer said. 'Rip's thinking more along the lines of battleships, cruisers.'

'Destroyers,' Old Cola said. 'Aircraft carriers. Like them, do you?'

'I don't know,' I said. 'I've never thought about it.'

'Ever seen a battleship, a carrier?' Wingate asked me.

I shook my head. *What the hell?* I thought.

'Want to?' Cola asked me. 'See one?'

'I don't know,' I said. *What the hell?*

'Sure, he does,' Homer said. 'This particular young fellow? Full of red pepper and beans? Full of the spirit of adventure?'

'Which we know he is,' Cola said. 'Hell-raiser that he is, all that energy. Energy, that's it. This valley ain't anywhere near big enough to hold him and all his energy.'

'He's getting ready to bust out of it like it's a cheap shirt,' Homer said.

'He needs a larger field of endeavour,' Wingate said.

'That's it,' Cola said. 'That's what it is.'

'Kind of young fellow the Navy was invented for, ain't he?' Homer said.

What?

'You've heard the saying,' Wingate said. 'Join the Navy, see the world? You can't beat that, can you?'

'You were an Army man, I thought,' Cola said to him.

'Same difference,' Wingate said. 'Either way, point's the same. Shipping out, is the point. Going away.'

'You need to go away,' Cola told me.

'You need to move on,' Homer said.

'The hell I do,' I said. 'Who says I do?'

'Who says, you're asking?' Wingate answered me. 'Everybody. Fact is, you're getting to be a pain in the neck. Did you do that with Morison's flagpole?'

'I don't know what you're talking about,' I said.

'You damned well do,' Cola said.

'You and your buddies,' Wingate said. 'Cooper. Tucker. Those boys.'

'If you've got trouble with my buddies,' I said, 'then talk to them.'

'We're talking to you,' Wingate said.

Cola had made a fire in the stove. Now he got to his feet and went to the stove. He opened the door and had a look at the fire. He dropped in a couple of sticks of wood from the box beside the stove. Then he reached around the stove and came up with an iron rod of some kind, like a poker, I thought. He shoved it into the fire and left it there. He came back to the table.

'We're making a friendly suggestion,' Homer said.

'Join the Navy, see the world,' Cola said. 'Or, the Army, Air Force, Marines, Coast Guard. Something else. It don't matter. Could be anything.'

'But move on,' Wingate said. 'Get yourself gone, at least for a couple of years – three, four.'

'Time to think,' Homer said.

Navy tour's three, ain't it?' Cola asked.

'Time to reflect,' Wingate said.

'And if I don't?' I asked.

The three of them sat there for a long moment, looking at me, saying nothing. Then Homer and Cola each looked at Wingate. Wingate sighed. 'Just full of piss and vinegar,' he said.

Cola got up again and went to the stove. He used a glove to pick up the poker he had left sticking out of the fire door. He held up the poker, looked at it, and put it back in the fire.

41

'We can do this in a couple of different ways,' Cola said.

'Do what?' I asked the three of them. 'Which ways? Who is it's behind you?'

'Nobody,' Cola said.

'Everybody,' Homer said.

'The valley,' Cola said.

'The valley,' Wingate said. 'We're here for the valley. It's the valley's behind us.'

'Whether they know it or not,' Cola said.

'Whether they like it or not,' Homer said.

'You mean you're here because you're sheriff?' I asked Wingate.

'No,' Wingate said. 'This ain't part of that. Not at all. This is another kind of thing.'

'A private thing, you could say,' Homer added.

'The real thing,' Wingate said.

'What do you think?' Cola asked me.

'I'll have to see,' I said.

'Do that,' Wingate said.

'We'll help you,' Homer said. 'We'll help you see.'

'Help?' I asked. 'When?'

'Now,' Homer said.

'We've got something to help you keep your mind on business,' Cola said.

'A reminder,' Wingate said.

Cola went back to the stove. He pulled the iron poker from the firebox. He blew on the end that had been in the fire. The end was a short, square piece of bar iron stock that had been heated in the fire until it was the dark red of some apples. The poker was not a poker. I knew what it was. Cola handed it to Wingate.

'Okay,' Cola said. 'Ready?'

He and Homer stood and moved to either side of my chair. Wingate brought the iron from the stove.

'Stand up, now,' Wingate said. I stood.

'Drop them,' Homer said. I unbuckled my belt and let my trousers and underwear fall.

'Get down over the table,' Homer said. 'Do you want us to hold you?' I shook my head and bent over the table. I could just see Homer and Cola at my sides. I couldn't see Wingate, behind me with the iron, but I could hear him.

'Here you go,' he said.

I passed out, must have. I didn't feel anything until I found myself in my car with Cola driving, following the lights of Wingate's truck ahead, on the dirt road that went back down Mount Nebo. I felt it then, all up and down of my right flank. Old Cola was talking. He was happy.

'Welcome back,' he said. He sounded like your surgeon right after you've come out of the gas. 'Don't worry. You're fine. You stood it pretty well. Now it's done. You got your reminder. I hope it works.'

'It will,' I told him.

Soon as my poor butt scabbed over, I was at the Navy recruiting office in Rutland. Then, now, and forever, if I twist around as far as I can go, or use a mirror, I can see Cola's mark, Wingate's reminder, the branded letters D F K. Nobody else has seen them, nobody else knows they're there. Well, Clemmie's seen them. I told her they stood for DELTA FORCE KARL, a secret unit of the Navy that I'd served in but was sworn never to talk about. Did she believe that? Probably not, but she didn't follow up on it, either, at least she hasn't yet.

More than once I have wondered why I let them do that to me, why I let them brand me like a calf. Back there at Cola's camp that night, I could have broken out and run. I could have fought them; at least I could have tried. It never occurred to me. Something about Wingate – the others, too, but especially Wingate. You didn't run from Wingate. You

43

didn't fight him. You knew you couldn't, and, then, anyway, you found you didn't want to. *We're here for the valley*, Wingate said. That was that.

D F K. Wingate said what my reminder really stands for is DAMN FOOL KID.

5
Everything in Families

It was my big brother, Paul, who first brought me the news that Clemmie and Jake might be involved. Thanks a lot, Paul. Though how could he have kept quiet about the business once Wendy, his miserable wife, had got a hold of it? Wendy, who loved nothing more than distress and sorrow, her own and others'? Wendy, whom our mother called The Undertaker? Wendy, who came up to me in the store one day around this time, looking like she was about to break down crying, took my hand in both of hers, peered up into my eyes, and said, 'Paul and I are so, so sorry, Lucian.' You'd have thought one of us had died – maybe both.

'You and Clemmie need some couples time,' Wendy told me another day.

'What kind of time?' I asked her.

'Couples time,' Wendy said. 'I read about it in one of my magazines. You need to go away together, take a vacation. Go to a new place, a romantic place, where you can fall in love all over again. Paul and I did it four or five years ago.'

'Where did you go?'

'Montreal.'

'Great,' I said, 'but that wouldn't work for Clemmie and me.'

'Why wouldn't it?'

'Jake don't speak French.'

Wendy looked at me, her eyes narrowed. 'What?' she said.

That's our Wendy: not a fun fair, not always quick to find the humour. If our mother thought Clemmie lacked brains, she thought Wendy was barely human.

But, really: Jake and Clemmie? Clemmie and Jake? Really? Jake's not far off my age. For sure there's no way he's a kid anymore, to go all night. And then, our mother's right: in the brains department, Jake's no hurricane. What do they talk about when they're not having at each other? He ain't smart enough for checkers. Must be they watch a lot of TV.

'I thought that was a high-school thing, Jake and Clemmie,' Paul said. 'I thought that was ancient history.'

So did I. I knew Clemmie had gone around with Jake in school, at least I guess I knew. I'm not sure. I was in my last year when they were just starting as freshmen. I knew their names, but that was it. By the time Clemmie and I got together, she and Jake had long since gone their separate ways. Jake was just another young fellow in town, and that's what he would have stayed – if not for me.

Fact is, I'm the one who got Clemmie and Jake started again. Sad, but true. I might as well have locked them up together in a broom closet. Wingate had retired, I was sheriff, I needed a new deputy to replace myself. Jake applied for the job. He's a big, strapping fellow, he appeared to be in his right mind, he had no criminal record, he was willing to work for the money I could pay him. You can't beat all that. I took him on.

Mistake. I had reckoned without Jake's IQ. A good deal of a rural deputy sheriff's time is spent in what we call patrolling, which really means driving around trying to stay awake. Jake was on top of patrolling well enough; but beyond it, he struggled. For example, traffic control. Deputies are called on to direct traffic on the roads from time to time. It don't seem like a big job – it ain't a big job – but it's a job that needs to be done a certain way. Otherwise, the result is confusion and unhappiness. Jake never got the hang of traffic work. I'm not sure he knew his left from his right. The time I put him on the Fourth of July parade in Cardiff, I placed him in front of the bank. The Antique Auto club from Brattleboro was coming down the main street. At the bank, they were to hold up so the Fire Department could enter the parade from the cross street. Jake somehow got fouled up and waved the lead firetruck ahead, causing a T-bone collision that brought the festivities to a standstill for an hour and cost a couple of insurance companies, probably, close to ten grand. I still hear about it.

I had to let Deputy Jake go, then, but not before Clemmie had gotten a good look at him. Nobody ever said Jake didn't turn out well in his sheriff's department uniform, and what with that, and Clemmie, no doubt, thinking of the old days when she and Jake were young and in love, and one thing and another – well, who knows how these things work? Suffice to say, there they were, Clemmie and Jake; and there as well, to tell me all about them, to make sure I was right up to date, were Paul and Wendy.

Paul's come along very well. He's the superintendent of schools for our district. Started as a math teacher, moved up, moved sideways, moved up again – now he's the head of the whole shop. No reason he shouldn't be state school commissioner someday, or better. But all Paul does, all day, every day, as far as I can tell, is read reports and go to meetings. I couldn't do that. I especially couldn't do the meetings. I'd rather write up speeders and stop fights, thank you very much.

Paul and I get on fine, as long as we don't get on too much. Paul's a baseball fan. He tries to go to our district's big games whenever he can. He enjoys it, and plus, it ain't a bad thing for the superintendent to be seen at the ball games, so everybody knows he's a regular type of fellow and not like some kind of royalty, intoxicated by the power and authority of his high position.

'Guess who I saw at the game the other night?' Paul asked me.

'Babe Ruth.'

'Clemmie. She was at the Springfield game. I didn't know Clemmie was a ball fan.'

I didn't, either. 'Sure,' I said. 'She loves it.'

'She was with Jake Stout,' Paul said. 'I didn't know Jake was a ball fan.'

'I guess he must be.'

'Though they weren't paying all that much attention to the game,' Paul said. 'I mean, the game on the field.'

After Paul had been kind enough to tip me about Clemmie and Jake, it didn't take long for certain signs and signals to show themselves. You can keep your eyes closed as long as you like, but if you open them, you can't help but see. Clemmie began not to be there when I got home at suppertime. She'd go for dinner and the movies with her cousin Amanda in Brattleboro and get home at three a.m. (Movies let out at nine.) Then she discovered another cousin, Marcia, in Massachusetts, who was a new one on me but who seemed to take a good deal of visiting – overnight visiting.

Clemmie and Jake didn't always do their business out of town, either. One day I got a call about a pair of vehicles abandoned along a road – really more of a trail – way to hell and gone back in the woods on Round Mountain. I drove up there and found the spot, a turn-out beside a power line cut. The vehicles were there, but they weren't abandoned. They were Clemmie's Accord and Jake's truck. Nobody was around. It looked to me like Clemmie and Jake had gone into the woods for a little privacy. Picnic, it looked like, or hunting mushrooms. What did I do? I pulled in behind their vehicles and turned off the truck's engine. I got out, didn't slam the truck's door, left it open. I started into the woods, going quietly, carefully, looking ahead and to either side. The power line cut was to my left, and on the edge of the clearing stood a big pine. I stopped walking. Clemmie and Jake were on the other side of that pine, maybe ten feet from me. I could hear them. First thing I heard was the hiss of a beer being opened: *pffft.* Then I heard Clemmie say, 'Thank you.' Jake said something I couldn't catch. Then Clemmie said, 'Oh, my goodness.' There was some rustling. Then Clemmie said, 'Ouch.' Jake said something. 'On my shoulder,' Clemmie said. 'No, behind.' More rustling. 'That had better not be a tick,' Clemmie said.

I'd found Clemmie and Jake. What was I going to do now? I didn't know. I didn't know what I was going to do until I saw myself do it. Nothing. I did nothing. I turned around and went back the way I'd come, quietly, carefully. I got to my truck, got in, started up, backed around, and drove out of there. I crept out of there, as though I had been the one who'd got caught, not Clemmie and Jake. Does that surprise you? It did me. But what else was I going to do? What else?

A couple of days later, I went out to Addison's. Clemmie's his daughter, after all, ain't she? I told Addison about the missed meals, the movies, the cousin in Massachusetts, the picnic.

'Is that right?' Addison said.

'She's having an affair with this fellow,' I said.

'What do you know?'

'She's cheating on me.'

'You don't mean it.'

'She's screwing Jake Stout.'

'No,' Addison said. 'Really?'

***

Paul says Wendy says Clemmie's taken up with Jake because she's restless. She's restless because she's dissatisfied. She's dissatisfied with me. Her husband's in the wrong line of work. I guess I should have gone out and become a doctor or a lawyer or a big businessman or maybe even a school Superintendent. What's the matter with me? Poor Clemmie.

And ain't it funny the way everything in families bounces off everything else, like in billiards? 'Paul and I are so, so sorry,' Wendy tells me. They're sorry for Clemmie, because she's restless. They're sorry for me, because of my low-class work, and now because of all this Jake business. Then, going farther back, and always handy when something to feel sorry for is needed, they're sorry for the both of us, because we don't have any kids. Well, so we don't. You'd think if Clemmie and I didn't mind that, Paul and Wendy wouldn't, either, but no: it seems to trouble them.

It shouldn't. They've covered our lack, themselves, and not just in baby-making, not just in quantity, but in quality still more. Paul and Wendy's son, Paul, Jr., goes to M.I.T. He's a genius. We're just waiting to see whether he'll turn out to be the kind of genius that invents things, or the kind that blows things up. Either way, Paul and Wendy have kids enough for two couples, easily. For kids, we're on their ticket. No chance Paul, Jr., will end up being a Grade B cop in the foothills. No chance he'll have a restless wife, the way Paul says Wendy says I have.

Truth is, our mother probably thinks the same way. She don't have a high opinion of the sheriff's office, never has. 'Let me see if I've got this straight,' she said once. 'You're going to spend the rest of your life right here, pulling over speeders, breaking up fights, directing traffic, and having philosophical discussions with Ripley Wingate. Is that it? You're joking, right? Tell me you're joking.'

6

The Elephants' Graveyard

I decided to take a ride out to Dead River, to Cola's shop. For a week, the Chairman had called every day. Yesterday, he'd called twice. What about Terry St. Clair? What had I done? What had I learned? What was I going to do next? What kind of sheriff was I, anyway?

So much for Chairman Steve. Meantime, nobody had seen Terry in over a week. The dumb kid had vanished. Maybe you couldn't blame him, but it didn't make my job any easier.

Dead River Settlement was five houses, two trailers, and an abandoned sawmill, gathered around a crossroads in the northwest corner of Gilead township. There was no post office, no store, and at this time two of the houses stood empty. Cola's shop was a cinder-block building a little out of the village, or hamlet, or whatever you call a tiny place like that. A sign out front said BROWN'S AUTO REPAIR, but it was no more than half true. Cola was in the business of working on cars, but his last name was Hitchcock, not Brown, he had bought the place years ago from a fellow named Churchill, and neither he nor anybody else had any idea who Brown was or might have been, or when.

The shop was two bays with a little office to the side where you waited for the work on your vehicle to get done. By the look of the premises outside, some customers had waited a long time. There was an open dirt yard in front, but to either side of the building, and behind it going back into the woods, wrecks and junkers of one kind and another sat in different stages of decay. Cola had an old fire truck, he had two school buses, a VW beetle, a bulldozer, three or four snow machines, and at least seven Ford Pintos. None of these ran, most would never run again, and around and behind them other dead vehicles, as well as axles, tyres, rims, fenders, chassis, seats, doors rusted away among the ragweed and the thistles. At the rear of the lot, partly hidden in the woods, was what was left of a Piper Cub that had crashed into Diamond Mountain in about 1960. Of course, it had ended up at Cola's. Where else would it go? Half garage, half scrap-metal shop, half junkyard, Cola's place looked like the Last Days of the Dinosaurs. It looked like the elephants' graveyard.

Terry St. Clair worked as Cola's helper, or he had. If you were looking for Terry, Cola's was where you might start.

When I drove up, Cola was sitting outside in the sun, having a beer. I pulled my truck up right in front of him and turned off my engine.

'If it ain't Matt Dillon,' Cola said.

'How's Cola?' I asked him. 'You keeping busy?'

'Killing myself. You want a cold one?'

'Not today. I'm looking for Terry. He here?'

'Terry?' Cola asked. 'Terry ain't been around for, oh, a week–ten-days. Not since he met with his mishap. You knew about that.'

'Heard he got caught in a baler.'

'That's what I heard, too. Tough break on the kid.'

'Worked here, didn't he?'

'Call it work,' Cola said.

'For how long?'

'Couple of years, on and off.'

'How did he do?'

'Not great, not terrible. Showed up, mostly. I don't ask for much more. At least, I don't generally get much more. I never had any trouble to speak of with Terry.'

'I heard he stole.'

'Not from me,' Cola said.

''Course,' I said, 'if he had, you wouldn't necessarily know it,' but Cola shook his head.

'He never stole from me,' he said again.

'Knew better than to, maybe,' I said.

'Maybe. What do you want with Terry?'

'The Chairman is taking an interest,' I said.

Cola blinked. 'You mean Roark?' he asked.

I nodded.

'What do you mean by "interest"?'

'The Chairman knows Terry,' I said. 'Thinks the world of him. Terry worked for him too, time to time, I guess. It was the Chairman found him the night he got hurt.'

'So?'

'The Chairman don't believe Terry had an accident,' I said. 'He thinks somebody cut him up.'

'So what if they did? What's it to Roark? Why's it his business?'

'You know the Chairman,' I said. 'Everything's his business. He don't believe it about the baler. He's after me to find out what really happened. He wants an investigation.'

'What kind of an investigation?' Cola asked.

'Find Terry, get him to talk. He's disappeared. Follow his trail. Talk to his family, his friends, his enemies. Run around. What I'm doing here. An investigation.'

'Okay,' Cola said. He got to his feet and stepped up to my window, where he leaned right in at me. A thing about Cola was that he had his eyes different colours. One was kind of hazel, the other a pale grey-blue, the colour of a frozen pond. He had the eyes of two different people, and that always stopped you for a second. Cola was a good fellow, but you were careful with him, in part because of those eyes. Which eye should you look at? Which one was right?

Cola held his gaze steady on me. 'Well, Lucian,' he said, 'if the Chairman wants an investigation, then we'd better give him one, hadn't we?'

'We?' I asked.

'You,' Cola said.

***

From Cola's, I drove clear across the county, to Cumberland Corners, where Terry's parents lived. His mother worked at the store there, so I'd probably miss her. That suited me. Anna St. Clair was a woman who'd been born pissed off and was now, in middle age, plain, flat furious. You tried to keep clear of her. You tried to deal with her husband, Terry's father, Stan.

I parked in front of St. Clairs'. Stan was around back splitting his winter's firewood with a sledgehammer and a steel wedge. I couldn't see him, but I could hear him hit the wedge with his hammer: *brink, brink, brink* – then, *brinnng*, when the chunk popped open. I went around the house.

Stan saw me. He set his hammer down head-first beside his block and waited.

'Look at you,' I said. 'Hard at work as always. Don't you ever lay off?'

But Stan wasn't buying at the candy counter today. 'What do you want?' he asked. Then, 'If you want Terry, he ain't here.'

'You know where he is?' I asked. 'I just want to ask him a couple of questions.'

'What questions? What's he done wrong?'

'Nothing that I know about. I just want to talk to him about his accident, what happened to him.'

'He told you what happened,' Stan said. 'Look, Lucian, look what the kid's been through already. He didn't do nothing. He's the victim, like. He just wants to get on with his life. Get over this, get his arm healed up, get his new hook or whatever they're going to give him, and get on.'

'What everybody wants,' I said. 'Do you know where he is?'

'Maybe I do, maybe I don't,' Stan said. 'Either way, if you think I'm telling you where he is, you're crazy.'

'I didn't ask you where he is. I asked you if you know where he is. I've just been to Cola's. Cola hasn't seen him since he got hurt.'

'Cola?' Stan asked. 'I ain't surprised Cola ain't seen him. Are you?' I didn't answer him, and Stan went on. 'I told you, I ain't saying any more. Not to you, not to Cola, not to nobody. Okay? I don't know where Terry is, and if I did, I wouldn't tell you. Ask Mr. Roark.'

'Roark?' I said. 'Wait a minute. Have you talked to Roark? The Chairman?'

'He's called,' Stan said. 'He's asked about Terry. He's Terry's boss, too. You keep after us, I might just talk to him. I might just tell Mr. Roark about how you come out here harashing Terry. Anna hears you've been here, she'll go batshit – more batshit than she usually is, I mean.'

'I'm doing what, to Terry?'

'Harashing,' Stan said. 'Harassing. You know. Steve Roark knows Terry. He's on Terry's side, on our side. You're god-damned right I'll tell him you were here doing – whatever.'

'Okay, you made your point,' I told Stan. 'You see Terry, ask him to give me a call, that's all he has to do, is call me, one time. Will you do that?'

'I ain't sure,' Stan said. 'Now, if you don't mind? Anna'll be home for lunch any minute.'

'Say no more,' I said. 'I'm going. I'm practically gone. Don't work too hard.' I left him. All right. That had gone pretty well. Would Stan tell Chairman Steve I'd been by? I'd bet he would, or his wife would. Did they think to go over my head, to get me in trouble with the Chairman on account of looking for Terry?

Well, I hoped so.

***

Back at my office, I fired my last round at the Terry-Roark business. I put in a call to Lieutenant Dwight Farrabaugh, the commander of the Vermont state police barracks in White River, and my one-time boss. Dwight was my window on up-to-date law enforcement. At the sheriff's department, we're lucky to have sixteen tyres for our four cruisers, but at the VSP, Dwight's got the whole bag of tricks.

'Terry St. Clair?' Dwight asked me. 'Sure, I know Terry. We've done a fair amount of business with Terry, one time and another. Petty theft, mostly, if I recall. You want a circular on Terry? You mean the whole country?'

'That's right,' I said.

'Why?' Dwight asked. I told him about Terry's injury, about seeing him in the clinic, how he seemed to have disappeared, how we needed police and others to watch out for him. 'Can you do that?' I asked Dwight.

'Sure, I can do it. But, again, why?'

'I just told you. He's missing. Nobody's seen him in a week. More.'

'So what?' Dwight said. 'You're not giving me a reason. You know how these things go, Lucian. A hook, I need a hook. Where's the hook? What's he done, Terry, besides getting his wing clipped? What laws has he broken? Is he a fugitive from justice?'

'Not exactly.'

'Lucian?'

'Yes?'

'Something's going on here, isn't it? You're getting some kind of heat, aren't you?'

'Could be,' I said.

Dwight had always been a man who understood his job and was good at it, had survived and even advanced in it, because he knew police work is like farming: the job is never done, it can't be; whatever you do, it's still ahead of you; you can never get ahead of it. Therefore, you do your best and hope it don't make you too crazy.

'Okay,' Dwight said. 'You've got your BOL. It won't find Terry for you. I hope it does whatever else you need it to.'

'I'm much obliged,' I said

'Funny, ain't it?'

'What?'

'Oh, guys like that,' Dwight said. 'You can't get them lined up right. You never can. Like with Terry: no sooner do you lose the little fucker fair and square than you find yourself out beating the bushes trying to get him back.'

7

The Look-See

Not wanting to get into another of our welterweight bouts with Clemmie, I gave it a week before I stopped back out by our place with the list of jobs she'd wanted done. I picked a day when Clemmie and her cousin Amanda had gone to New Hampshire to shop. At least, that's where Addison said she said she'd be. Maybe it was a lie. Maybe Clemmie and Jake were burning up the Super-8 in Brattleboro. As long as she wasn't home, what did I care?

At the house, I found the place deserted except for Stu the cat, who was sitting in the sun on the front porch waiting for me. I got my toolbox and went up onto the porch.

'Hey, Stu,' I said. 'Thought you were missing.'

Stu got to his feet and came to rub his head and flanks against my ankles. He was purring away like a fat fluffy tea kettle.

'Good to see you, too, Stu,' I said. 'I guess you and the Don didn't meet up out there, after all. You were lucky, Stu. Your mom was worried. We both were.'

Stu led the way to the kitchen door. We went in. A pane in one of the kitchen windows had been broken. These were double-hung, six-over-six wooden sash, and the busted pane was in the lower sash. This was the biggest job on Clemmie's list, so I started with it.

Believe it or not, re-glazing simple windows is work I have always enjoyed. If you take care and go slow, it's a job that's almost impossible to screw up. And plus, when you've finished, the sense of having made a real improvement, even though it's only a small improvement, is strong. New, clean, tight glass makes the world on both sides of the window look well-cared-for, makes it look good, even if it ain't.

Stu jumped up on the kitchen counter and sat, watching me work. I opened my toolbox and took out my little nail-puller, which I used carefully on the window casing to take off the narrow pieces of wood on either side that kept the sash in place. I put them aside. I then dismounted the sash with the broken pane and laid it down on the kitchen counter, outside-up.

'Here's where we could go wrong, Stu,' I said. 'But we won't. We're too smart.'

I took the upper sash out of the window, too. Nothing on it was broken, but with the lower sash removed, not much held the upper in place. Many a window job has gone from little to big in a hurry when an unsupported upper sash has fallen. I stood the window safely on the floor to one side.

Then I set about removing the bits of jagged glass from the woodwork surrounding the broken pane. When they were cleared away, I took my needle-nose pliers and pulled out the little steel glazier's points that had held the glass pane in place. I saved the points. There were eight of them. When they were gone, I used a short-bladed knife to scrape and cut away the dried, hardened putty from the narrow shelf milled into the woodwork where the new glass would lie.

I was about ready to prepare the woodwork for the new pane. First, I went lightly over the shelf with fine sandpaper. Then I got out my little artist's paint brush and a can of linseed oil. I stroked a thin coat of oil on the shelf.

'Stu, my boy,' I said. 'You don't put the linseed to her, you ain't doing a job.'

While the oil was soaking in, I got out the new pane of glass I'd picked up at the hardware. I don't try to cut my own glass; never had much luck with that.

'Let the pros do it,' I told Stu. 'They're getting paid. You and I ain't.'

I got the putty out of my toolbox and laid down a bead of putty on the prepared shelf, smoothing and evening it out with a putty knife. Then I carefully placed the new glass pane on the bead and pressed it down, seating it gently but firmly. I replaced the steel points. You don't try to tap them in. Do that, sooner or later you break the glass. Instead, you shove them into the woodwork using a screwdriver. When the points were in, I sealed around the woodwork with another bead of putty and used the putty knife to trim away any excess putty and to bevel the putty neatly outside. Then I cleaned the glass, hung the two sashes back where they belonged, and replaced the little keeper strips to either side. I swept and straightened up the counter.

'Well, Stu,' I said. 'We've got the faucet and the light still to go, but we can do them another time. For now, I'm calling it good. What about you? You ready to call it good? Okay, then. We're off the clock. Let's have a little look-around. You with me? Just a little look-see?'

I went to the pantry where Clemmie keeps the mops, the brooms, the vacuum cleaner, the trash, and so on. Who did I think would be hiding in there, Jake? 'Course not. Anyway, he wasn't. I opened the fridge: plenty of PBR, which would be for Jake, and a bottle of white wine, Clemmie's. Eggs, milk, a package of bacon. I thought of having a beer for myself, but no. I'm a snoop, I'm a – whatever the word Addison called me was – a cuckold. I'm those things and more, much more, and worse. But I ain't a thief.

Stu and I left the kitchen and went into the living room. 'Don't worry, Stu,' I said. 'We ain't spying, here. This is our place. It ain't spying when it's your place.'

The hell it ain't, but never mind.

Everything was neat and tidy in the living room: cold fireplace swept out, no empty glasses or the like, no newspapers or magazines. No clothes.

'For a big fellow, our Jake don't leave much of a footprint, does he, Stu?' I said. 'Let's try upstairs.'

We went up to the second floor. Bathroom right at the top of the stairs. Bath towel hanging on the bar in there, slightly damp. I opened the medicine cabinet. Well, well. Can of shaving cream and a razor. Blades. Toothbrush. Eye drops. Aspirin. Also a bottle of pills with a prescription label made out to Jacob Stout: take as directed for hypertension. Hypertension. That's high blood pressure.

'I ain't surprised, Stu,' I said. 'She's gaining on him.'

We went on to the spare bedroom, but you could tell from the doorway that nothing had been going on in there. Two of my old deputy's uniforms were hanging in the closet, nothing else.

Time for the main event, now. 'Let's do her, Stu,' I said, and, with Stu leading the way, we went into the main bedroom, Clemmie's and my bedroom. Some call it the 'master' bedroom. Why, I wouldn't know. Not in this house, anyway.

We found everything shipshape. Clothes hung up, the forest of little bottles, jars, and tubes on Clemmie's dressing table in good order, the bed neatly made. Stu jumped up onto the bed and settled down in his usual place. As a rule, he slept between Clemmie and me, about at our knees.

'You still got your old spot, these days, Stu?' I asked him. 'Me, neither.'

I quickly checked the windows. Clemmie might not be back for hours, but again, she might walk in at any time. I left the window. I dropped to all fours and looked under the bed. Clemmie's slippers, and a button. I didn't touch them. I got to my feet and went to the closet. Clemmie's dresses, Clemmie's shoes, my winter uniforms – and, up on a shelf, a big Stetson hat, western-style, cream colour, and evidently brand new. I reached it down and turned it over. Inside, J.S. embossed on the wide leather hatband. Custom work, here. No Wal-Mart's. Not even Jake would get a hat like that for himself, for sure not with a fancy printed band. Clemmie had to have given it to him.

'You know what they say about cowboy hats and haemorrhoids, don't you, Stu?' I said. Stu looked at me from his place on the bed. 'Sooner or later, every asshole gets one,' I said.

The dresser. The bottom drawer was my drawer. I found a couple of my sweaters and my heavy shirts, woollen socks. Buried under the socks was Wingate's old U.S. Army .45 pistol from World War Two. He'd given it to me when he retired.

'I'd think you'd want to hang onto it,' I said to Wingate at the time.

'What for?' Wingate asked me. 'I've got no use for it now.'

'Well, then, just as a souvenir?'

'A souvenir? You mean of the war? There's nothing about the war I care to remember.'

Clemmie had the top two dresser drawers. In the lower one, Clemmie's straw jewel box. I opened it. Clemmie loves earrings. Can't have too many earrings. Who can keep track of them all? Not me, but I didn't see any that I was sure were brand new.

'Think about it, Stu,' I said. 'Jake gets Clemmie. He gets a free place to live. He even gets a fancy new hat. Clemmie don't even get a new pair of earrings. It's a man's world, ain't it?' I shut the jewel box. In the remainder of the drawer was half a mile of underwear. I searched through it. What was I doing? Was I no more than a nasty little boy? No better than a peeper?

'Shame on us, Stu,' I said.

We went back downstairs and into the kitchen. I packed up my toolbox and got ready to take off. Stu sat by the kitchen door and watched me.

'Well, Stu,' I said. 'Sure looks like Jake's moved in, don't it? We wanted evidence, we got it. Trouble is, we can't do much with it, on account of your mom's not to know we've got it, on account of we got it on the sly. It's what you call a bind, ain't it?'

Stu and I left the kitchen and went out on the porch. 'Take her easy, Stu,' I said. 'Your mom gets home, I wasn't here, right? You never saw me. Oh, and Stu: stay out of the woods, okay? That big fellow's out there. Just because you missed him this last time don't mean he ain't.'

I went to my truck. Stu was on the porch where he had been when I'd driven up. I backed around and drove out down our lane to the road. It's a good thing I moved when I did, too, because before I was a mile down the road, here came Clemmie on her way home I waved. She waved.

8

Calamity Jane

I was breaking in a new deputy that summer, the sheriff's department's first female officer. Addison called her Calamity Jane.

Deputy Olivia Gilfeather was a serious piece of business: rangy, red-haired, and six feet high, more than an inch taller than me. She was thirty-seven, a ten-year veteran of the Marine Corps with three deployments overseas in one or another of those Godforsakistan places we seem unable to stay out of these days. In the Marines she had had the rank of Lance Corporal. If you asked her what her military duty had been, she said, 'Security,' and had nothing to add on the subject. In fact, she didn't have much to add on any subject. Lance Corporal Gilfeather was serious business in more than size.

'Olivia?' I said when she interviewed for the deputy job. 'What do people call you, Livy?'

'They call me Lance Corporal,' she said.

'Are you married?'

'Divorced.'

'Kids?'

'No.'

'From around here, originally?'

'No.'

'Where?'

'Upstate.'

'Burlington? St. Johnsbury? Montpelier?'

'No.'

You get the idea: not much of a tail-wagger; not a forest fire of charm. I said I was breaking in a new deputy, but it might have been the new deputy that was doing the breaking.

Was I happy to have a female deputy? I'll admit I was not. It wasn't what I was used to. The fact is, though, I didn't have much choice. Our department had been short a deputy for nearly a year. Recruitment was not easy. Applicants weren't plentiful. I never could understand why. You would think thousands of bright, fit, dedicated young men would jump at a career that had them driving around alone in the dirtiest weather all over the hills and through the woods in a fleet of clapped-out Crown Vics; having to handle citizens in every extreme of crisis, misery, intoxication, insanity, and rage; obliged to buy much of their own equipment; putting in ten-, twelve-hour days as a regular thing; and getting compensation that was well within sight of the minimum wage. You'd think promising young fellows would be fighting for that, wouldn't you? Well, the evidence is, they ain't.

Therefore, Deputy Gilfeather, Olivia-call-me-Lance-Corporal, the leatherneck, Addison's Calamity Jane. Maybe she wasn't my fondest wish, but here she was. By brains and experience she was overqualified. (Certainly she was better qualified than, say, I was.) I hired her like a shot.

'Can you start tomorrow?' I asked her.

'Roger,' Lance Corporal Gilfeather said.

It was soon clear that, as an officer of the law, Deputy Gilfeather was made of different stuff from Jake Stout. As a new member of the sheriff's department, she was put on traffic control duty, just as Jake had been. But while Jake, directing traffic, would strut around and wave his arms and blow his whistle and generally carry on like a barnyard goose, snarling up everything in the process, Deputy Gilfeather controlled traffic the way a good working dog controls a flock of sheep. She did it by eye, by her look. She stood still and fixed oncoming motorists with a very particular gaze, a burning, piercing gaze that made them fall into line in a hurry. It was a pleasure to watch her.

'I guess you must have had traffic detail overseas, some, didn't you?' I asked her.

'No,' Deputy Gilfeather said.

***

In her first couple of weeks with the department, as we both had time, I drove Deputy Gilfeather up and down the valley showing her the places where the action was. A quarter to a third of our valley has, for all practical purposes, no people in it: it's woods, bogs, and mountain beaver meadows. In the rest, there are certain venues, well known to all, that keep on making business for local law enforcement. It helps to learn them off early; it saves work. I mean, if you're hunting rats, you don't right off go looking for them in church, though if you did you'd probably find a few. No, if it's rats you're after, you start at the dump.

So, the deputy and I took a sheriff's department cruiser and drove out to the dead-end roads and remote campsites far back in the puckerbrush where the high school students went to drink beer and smoke dope in the few short hours when they weren't slaving away on their Latin and their Conic sections. We looked over the clearings deep in the woods where, among the dark and crowded firs, the Future Farmers of America kids grew pot for themselves and their friends.

We also called at the North Country Inn, on Route 10 near the county line. When we drove up, Fred Teachout was standing in front of the entrance. The inn was not looking its best that morning. Somebody had ripped the main door right out of the frame. The door was lying on the ground. Fred was a carpenter, evidently hired to repair the door. He was scratching his head. The parking lot was covered with broken glass, and an old Ram pickup was lying on its roof in the lot's corner, having flipped.

'I heard they had a heavy night,' Fred said.

'I heard the same,' I said. The deputy and I went inside, where we found Carl, the owner, working on the floor with a mop and bucket. Carl was sweating.

'All that blood's a bitch when it dries, ain't it, Carl,' I said.

'Ha, ha, Sheriff,' Carl said.

'This is Deputy Gilfeather,' I told Carl. 'She just joined the department. I thought I'd bring her out, introduce her. Tried to pick a time when things are calm, you know?'

Carl nodded at the deputy, who looked at him but didn't nod or speak.

'Carl puts on more fights in here than they do at Madison Square Garden, don't you, Carl?' I asked him.

'Ha, ha, Sheriff,' Carl said again. He spoke to the deputy. 'I don't put nothing on,' he said. 'I run an orderly place.'

'With a little help from us, and the state police, and the Eighty-second Airborne,' I said.

'Nice to meet you, deputy,' Carl said. 'Sorry you have to hurry away. Stop in again. Don't feel you have to bring the boss. Just stop in, any time.'

'Oh, she will,' I said. 'We both will. Count on it.'

Carl swung his mop and made his bucket on its little rollers pass too near our shoes. Time to go.

'Carl ain't a bad fellow,' I told the deputy as we drove away from the inn 'He's under a lot of occupational stress, there.

Dodging beer steins and shot glasses year in, year out – it grinds you right down.'

'Poor him,' the deputy said.

Another day, I took Deputy Gilfeather by the Sugar Maple Cabins. These were seven old-time tourist cabins and an office, on a lot that fronted on the two-lane, in what had been a likely spot before the highway was rerouted to the east. Now the Sugar Maple was on the cut-off and got no trade. Well, that wasn't quite right: there was still trade, but it was sparse, and some part of it was single ladies who rented cabins by the hour. When we drove up in the cruiser, there were vehicles in front of two or three of the cabins, but the place looked deserted.

The deputy and I went to the office. The door was open, but nobody was inside, and nobody answered when we rang the bell for service. We returned to the cruiser.

'Quiet place,' Deputy Gilfeather said.

'They're here,' I told her, 'but they're working.'

'Not all of them,' the deputy said. 'Look.'

I went around to where she stood on the other side of the vehicle. From there you could see three fellows running awkwardly away from the rear of the cabins, making for the woods. Two of them carried their pants, the third had evidently left his behind.

'Must be the cruiser spooked them,' I said. 'You see what was going on, though, right?'

'Roger,' Deputy Gilfeather said.

'Be aware of this place,' I said, 'but don't worry yourself about it. The Sugar Maple don't bother much. Oh, every so often one of the older customers will overdo it and go into cardiac arrest, but that's more a job for the EMTs.'

'Roger,' the deputy said.

I saved the best for last: Robbers' Roost Ranch, a big old place on the road to Diamond Mountain from the other side, in the town of Gilead. It had been built years and years ago to be a boarding house for men who worked on the logging railroad. Then it had been a school. Then it had been somebody's home. Now it was occupied by a semi-permanent population of habitual offenders, fugitives, vagrants, dealers, and general riffraff.

In addition to being a dormitory for evil-doers, Robbers' Roost was a kind of bazaar or marketplace for every kind of contraband. Street drugs, drugstore drugs, untaxed beer and liquor, cigarettes, stripped auto parts and sometimes the autos themselves, firearms of all kinds, TVs and other electronic gear originating elsewhere – all of it was for sale at the Roost.

Nobody knew exactly who owned the Roost. It might have been one of the large, grimy, long-bearded fellows whom Deputy Gilfeather and I found standing around out in front of the house, working on a truck. The Roost's inmates were a different proposition from Carl and the customers at the Sugar Maple. They were in another league. They had long since given up their amateur standing. Deputy Gilfeather evidently understood that. We left the cruiser and went across the road to the three at the truck. As we approached, the deputy let me get a little ahead of her, while she moved a couple of steps to my right. I took note of that.

There in front of the Roost, the three of them had left off whatever they were doing to the truck and watched the deputy and me come up.

'Hello. Boomer,' I said. 'Hello, Rick. Hello, Travis.'

The three didn't even nod. The oldest, Sidney Perkins, called Boomer, said, 'Help you?'

'I wanted to make you acquainted with our new deputy,' I told him. 'Boomer Perkins, Rick McCoy, Travis Hutchins, this is Deputy Gilfeather. I wanted you to meet her. Her to meet you.'

'So, we met her,' Boomer said. 'We met her, she met us, okay? We're busy.'

I laid my hand on the hood of the truck the three had been working on. 'Good-looking rig,' I said. 'You've got tags for it, of course.'

'Inside,' Boomer said. 'You want to see them?'

'No need at all,' I said. I turned to the deputy. 'Boomer here's a genius with an engine,' I told her. 'He can get anything started. Ain't that right, Boomer?'

Boomer was silent.

'Yes, it's something to see,' I went on. 'The Boomer's an artist, I mean it. And fast? Boomer can get you going in three, four seconds flat, most cars. Believe it or not. Right, Boomer?'

'Like I said, we're busy,' Boomer said.

'Anyone can see that,' I said. 'We'll let you get back to work. You ready?' I asked the deputy. She had held her place a little to my right, quartering Boomer and the others. We went back to the cruiser. Boomer and his crew watched us drive off.

'I saw you cover me, there,' I told the deputy.

'Roger,' Deputy Gilfeather said. 'Dirtbags.'

'It helps them to know we know them. Their names, where they are. It helps them reflect.'

'Roger.'

'You won't be in and out of here as much as you will Carl's,' I told Deputy Gilfeather. 'But you'll be here for worse. Don't ever go into the Roost alone. Always have back-up, at least two. You won't know what you'll find.'

'Yes, I will. Dirtbags.'

'Well, you're right about that,' I said. 'Truth is, this one place, just by itself? If I could get in here one time with a machinegun, a big can of DDT, and a gallon of kerosene? Just this place? I could bring the crime rate in this valley – in this whole end of the state – down seventy-five percent.'

'Why don't you, then?' Deputy Gilfeather asked me.

'Say what?'

'Do it,' she said. 'You know, get a team together, train, go in, do it, get out. Simple.'

That was the most talking I'd heard from the deputy since she'd joined up.

'It's simple, all right,' I said. 'But it ain't exactly according to what you'd call the law, is it?'

The deputy shrugged.

'Is it?' I asked her.

'Not all law, maybe,' the deputy said.

'*All* law? What other law is there?'

Deputy Gilfeather shrugged again. 'It depends,' she said.

'On what?'

'On what it takes. On what has to be done. On the situation.'

'Steady, there, Deputy. Stay in your lane. We don't get to pick our law,' I said. But I was thinking. Depends on what it takes, she'd said, hadn't she? Depends on the situation? Deputy Gilfeather might have a future up here, I was thinking. She just might.

Another thing I did to get Deputy Gilfeather briefed as we made our tours around the valley was to stop at the different town offices and show her to the town clerks. Town clerks are good people for the sheriff to be on the right side of. There are thirteen of them in our valley, and all of them are women in middle age. Why town-clerking should be a female job as much as it seems to be, I can't say for sure. How God made the world, it looks like. In any case, it was a break for Deputy Gilfeather, and for me. I knew each of our clerks was tickled that the sheriff now had a woman for a deputy. Did my hiring Deputy Gilfeather mean their sheriff was a more progressive, a more intelligent fellow than they had thought? Or did it mean only that he was the same old cave man as always, but now for some reason he wanted their good opinion? The town clerk ladies had different views on that, no doubt, but either way they all seemed pleased with Deputy Gilfeather – and (at least temporarily) pleased with me. Our visits to the town offices went along very well.

Or they did until we got to my own town, Cardiff. There, we left Mattie Thurston beaming like a fresh-baked apple pie, only to run into Stephen Roark, the Chairman himself, coming up the steps of the town hall.

He started right in, didn't even see the deputy. 'I've been looking for you, Sheriff,' he said. 'How is your investigation into Terry St. Clair's case going?'

'Going great,' I said. 'We've got all kinds of good leads.'

'What leads?'

'You know I can't tell you that, Mr. Roark,' I said. 'The investigation is active. It's ongoing. That's all I can say.'

'Bullshit,' the Chairman said. 'Nobody has seen Terry in a week or more. A week or more. Are you even aware of that, Sheriff?'

'I'm aware of that.'

'Do you know where he is?'

I didn't answer. Instead, I turned to the deputy. 'This is our new officer, Deputy Gilfeather,' I told the Chairman. 'Deputy, Mr. Roark is selectman chairman up here.'

The Chairman didn't so much as say hello. He took a quick look at the deputy. He shook his head. Then he said to me, 'Can I have a word, Sheriff?'

Deputy Gilfeather went back to the cruiser. The Chairman took me by the elbow and turned me away from the road. He stepped in close.

'Where did you get that Amazon?' he asked me.

'She applied.'

'You've hired her?'

'That's right.'

'Bad idea, Sheriff. She can't cut it. None of them can.'

I didn't say anything.

'I've made hundreds of hires, Sheriff. I've never seen it fail. Women don't do well in ranked, command organisations like yours. They aren't subordinate. They may seem to be, but they aren't. Never. They aren't team-players. They can't be. It's biological.'

'Is that right?'

'Yes, it is,' the Chairman said. 'You'll find out it is. You've made a mistake.'

'Could be, I guess,' I said. 'I made another one once – course, that was some years back.'

'I want you to find Terry St. Clair, Sheriff,' the Chairman said. 'I also want your written report on his assault. I want it this week.'

'I'll try.'

'Don't try, Sheriff. Do it.' He pushed past me and went on into the town hall.

In the cruiser, Deputy Gilfeather was silent.

'That was the Chairman,' I told her. 'He was in the military, like you.'

'Not like me,' the deputy said.

'No, I guess not. I hope not. Fair to tell you, though, he's got his doubts about you, the Chairman has. He don't think you're up to the job.'

'We'll see,' the deputy said.

'Don't worry, though,' I went on. 'The Chairman knows it ain't your fault. It's biological.'

'We'll see.'

'Let me worry about the Chair,' I said. 'He's my problem, he ain't yours.'

'If he's your problem, Sheriff, then he's my problem, too. I'm your deputy.'

'I appreciate that, Deputy,' I said.

'Roger,' Deputy Gilfeather said.

9

The Iron in Her

Paul was worried about our mother. He was worried about her, and because he was worried about her, everybody else had to be worried about her, too. 'Open your eyes, Little Brother,' Paul said. 'She can't go on the way she is. Living alone. She can't. You see she can't.'

'I see she can't go on living any other way,' I said. 'Can't. Won't. Same thing, with her.'

'Then we'll just have to make her,' Paul said. 'We'll just have to lay down the law.'

'You given any thought to who you're laying down the law *for*, here?'

'I know,' Paul said. 'I know, but we have to do it anyway.'

'Who does?'

'All of us. We've talked about it, you know. I've offered to have her live with Wendy and me. I've offered more than once. Paul Junior's in Cambridge, we've got the room. Not a chance of it, of course, not with how she and Wendy get along. Okay. So then I thought she'd go to you and Clemmie, when the time came. She always liked you best, anyway.'

'She did?'

'Sure, she did,' Paul said. 'She did, she does, and you know it.'

'No, I don't. But I wouldn't be surprised if it was so. I'm highly likeable.'

'The point is,' Paul said, 'Mom might have gone to you and Clemmie, but then you two have to go and split up. Thanks for nothing, Little Brother.'

'So what if we split up?' I asked Paul. 'No problem. Tell her to come ahead. She'll love the office. She can have the couch. I'll sleep on the floor. I don't mind, really I don't.'

'I'm not kidding, Lucian.'

'I know you're not.'

'Listen,' Paul said. 'I've been thinking. I want to take her to visit Steep Mountain.'

'Steep Mountain?'

'Steep Mountain. You know: the retirement place, up there. The care community.'

'I know what it is,' I said. 'I also know she'll never go there. So do you.'

'No,' Paul said. 'I mean just to visit. It's a nice place. She'll see that. She'll see it's not some kind of death house.'

'It ain't?'

'She'll do it, Lucian, she'll visit, if you come along. You have to come along. I just want her to have a look at the place. She doesn't have to decide.'

''Course, she don't have to decide. You've decided.'

'For her?' Paul said. 'I decided for Mom? You know better.'

I did. Our mother, Lorraine Hancock Wing, admitted to being fifty-seven, but was in fact several years older. Birthdays, if they were hers, didn't count, she reckoned. That was Mom. If she didn't want to have turned sixty, well, she wouldn't. She knew what she wanted, and if she didn't get it, if things didn't line up her way, she acted as if they had until they did – or something busted. A person with some iron in her. A strong person.

She'd had to be, I guess. She had been on her own her whole adult life. She had passed directly from girlhood to widowhood with nothing much in between. War does that for you. Our father, Lt. (jg) Bradley Wing, was a Navy combat flyer, based on the aircraft carrier *U.S.S. Ranger* in the Gulf of Tonkin. He was the bombardier/navigator of an A6 Intruder, the two-seat dive-bomber of the Vietnam War. One day in November 1969, Lt. Wing and his pilot launched from the *Ranger* on a bombing mission over the Ho Chi Minh Trail in Laos. They took ground fire. The pilot ejected and was quickly and safely recovered. No sign of Lt. Wing: no chute, no sight, no signal – no nothing. He was gone.

Today, Lt. (jg) Bradley Wing, is on the Navy's books as Missing in Action. The stonecutters stateside know better. You can find his name along with some fifty others on the granite marker in the middle of Cardiff Common, a memorial to the fallen in America's wars. He was twenty-two. Goodbye, Brad.

Our mother was nineteen. There were a number of young wives in our valley in the same spot in those years. That will get you grown up. It will get you grown up in a hurry. At least, it did Mom.

What Paul and I had of our father was ten or twelve photos and the few recollections of people who had known him. That by no means included Paul and me. Paul was only two or three when our father died, but at least our father had seen Paul. Mom had a snapshot of them together, our father in his uniform holding Paul in his blanket. That beat me. When our father died, I was still inside of Mom. Our father never saw me. I never saw him. Everybody used to tell me I looked like him, but I could never see it. From the photos, I thought he looked more like Paul, though not all that much, either, really.

Our mother, with one-and-three-quarters kids, had to start in putting things together by herself. She made it work, not always smoothly. She taught the little kids' school for a couple of years. It didn't go well. She hadn't the patience for it. 'They wouldn't mind,' she said of her first- and second-graders. 'They wouldn't mind, they wouldn't sit still, and they wouldn't shut up.' She worked in the store, she worked at the inn here in Cardiff. She started as a waitress, but that didn't last long. Soon, she was managing the inn for its owners, Mr. and Mrs. DeJonge. That didn't last too long, either. Patience was again an issue. Mom had about the same things to say about the inn's guests and patrons, and about Mr. and Mrs. DeJonge, as she had about the school kids. The DeJonges evidently thought that, since they owned the inn and paid our mother's salary, they should have some say-so over how the place was operated. Mom didn't see the need for that. She was the manager, wasn't she? Let her manage, then. For a number of years she worked at the post office.

Did she have men friends? None that Paul or I ever saw. A penniless widow with no skills and two little boys don't exactly draw big competition. And then, I can see how, Mom being who she is, not every fellow would have had what it took. I mean, who's in charge?

Always she lived in the little house down from the church, where she and her husband had barely begun to set up housekeeping. There, she had her strung-up morning glories in front and her garden in back. She tended her vegetables. She kept and cared for a line of dogs and a longer line of cats. She saw a lot of Paul and Wendy, though Wendy, she couldn't abide. She didn't see as much of me, though Clemmie helped her out with this and that. Our mother liked Clemmie, though she made fun of her as the airhead daughter of a rich trifler, which was the part she'd long since given to Addison. Did she really like me best, the way Paul said? I doubt it. Why would she?

Things were going along pretty well, then, the way I've said they generally do if you let them – until Mom fell down the stairs.

Good thing for her, Clemmie came over that morning to help her with her canning. Clemmie found our mother on the floor in the hallway, out cold. She called me, I called the ambulance, and we took off for the clinic. On the way Mom came to, insisted she was fine, and demanded to be taken home. We made her go ahead to the clinic, though, and she spent the day being watched over by the medics. They wanted to keep her overnight, but Mom said absolutely not. She'd been cooperative all day. That was more than enough of that. They let her go. She went on home. She was all right.

No, she wasn't.

***

It was shortly after Mom's fall that Clemmie called me at the office. This was a couple of weeks after I'd moved out. We hadn't spoken past Hello in that time, unless you count our occasional engagements in the ring. If Clemmie had anything to say to me, she went through Addison.

'Lucian, I'm sorry to be calling,' Clemmie said. 'I know you don't need to hear from me right now, but it's urgent. It's your mom. I'm worried about her.'

'Talk to Paul,' I told her. 'He's the one who's worried about Mom. It ain't me. I ain't worried. Talk to Paul.'

'I'm talking to you, Lucian,' Clemmie said. 'All right?'

Ding, went the bell.

'Talk away,' I said.

'I went there this morning to take her to the Grand Union, like I always do,' Clemmie said. 'She's always got the coffee on, and we always have a cup while she makes her list. So I walk in, and she's just sitting there in the kitchen, at the table. No coffee. No list. She's just sitting there looking at the wall. Staring at the wall. Doesn't say hello, doesn't get up. Just sits and looks. A very funny look.'

'Just because not everybody strikes up the band when you walk into the room don't mean there's anything to be worried about,' I told Clemmie.

'Let me finish, okay?' Clemmie said. 'So, I said to her, you know, "Hi, good morning." And she said, "Brad was here." And I said – well, I don't know – I guess I said, like, "Really? Brad, your husband? Right here? With you?" And your mom said, "Yes, he was here, but he couldn't stay. He had to go. They were calling him, he said." "Who was calling him?" I asked her. And she said she didn't know, he didn't say. Then she seemed to kind of shake herself. She got up from the table, and she said, "Oh, I'm sorry. What was I doing? Oh, I know. Wait a minute. I'll get the coffee going."'

'That was it?' I asked Clemmie.

'Yes, Lucian, that was it. Wasn't it enough?'

'Enough, what?'

'I do not believe you,' Clemmie said. 'Two hours ago, your mother was completely out of her mind. She thought she was talking to a dead person. She was in some kind of – I don't know. Some kind of break. Lord, do you not get that?'

'I get it. I don't get what you want me to do about it.'

'Well, something. Maybe she should see somebody.'

'Somebody, who?'

'Some doctor.'

'Oh,' I said. 'Well, I don't know. What's Jake think?'

'Jake? What's Jake got to do with it?'

'Well,' I said. 'I wouldn't want to make up my mind about anything in the medical department, you know, the psychological department, until I had the benefit of Jake's point of view. His education. His training.'

'You know what, Lucian?' Clemmie said. 'You know what? Fuck you.'

Click.

Ding. End of the round.

I knew Clemmie's next call would be to Paul. She and Paul would get together on deciding our mother needed help. Well, she did. Clemmie and Paul were right. If Mom thought she was getting visits from her long-dead flyboy husband after forty years, then she was cuckoo, for sure, and something had to be done. Now, I don't care what it is, my idea is and has always been, if something has to be done, don't do it. Nine times out of ten, it didn't have to be done, at all, and you're better off. But not this time, maybe. Even I had to admit that, though I didn't have to admit it to Clemmie.

Anyway, that's where we were. And therefore, Steep Mountain.

10
The Soft Path

Terry St. Clair broke out of hiding with a bang that looked for a minute like it was going to punch my ticket, and his – and his crazy mother's into the bargain. One of Dwight Farrabaugh's troopers thought he had spotted Terry at his parents' place. Our dispatch put it out, and Deputy Gilfeather, who was patrolling in Cumberland, started over there. I went from the office. The deputy ought to have beaten me to Terry, then, but she didn't know all the roads yet. She got a little lost. I was the first at St. Clairs'. For Terry and his mother, that was probably a good thing.

I found Terry in the front passenger's seat of the Taurus his mother, Anna, drove. Anna was behind the wheel. They were getting ready to leave in a hurry. No sign of Stan.

I pulled over to one side of the St. Clairs' lane and parked about twenty feet from Anna and Terry. I left my truck and started toward the Taurus, walking up the middle of the lane. As I approached, Anna started her engine. I came ahead. Anna put the car in gear and let it roll toward me. I could see Terry in the seat beside her. His left arm was still in a big bandage.

I halted. I held my hands up so Anna could see I wasn't armed. She stopped the Taurus, holding it with the brake. She stuck her head out the driver's window.

'Get out of my way, Sheriff.'

'I'm here to see Terry,' I told her.

'You'll leave my son alone,' Anna said. 'He's done nothing wrong. Now, get out of my way.'

Anna let up on the brake, and the Taurus rolled to a couple of feet in front of me, where she stopped it again. She leaned on the horn. I kept my place in front of her.

'I will run you down, Sheriff,' Anna said. 'Don't think I won't. I will protect my son.'

I looked to my right. With the action and the racket of Anna's horn, none of us had noticed Deputy Gilfeather. On arriving at the St. Clairs', a couple of minutes behind me, she had left her cruiser in the road and sprinted up the lane toward the Taurus. Now she stood at the driver's side window. Her service pistol, grasped in both hands, combat-style, she held levelled on Anna St. Clair's head, no more than five feet from her.

'I've got her, Sheriff,' Deputy Gilfeather said quietly. 'I've got them both.'

Anna had seen her now, but she didn't react. 'Sheriff?' she said. 'For the last time, get out of my way. I will run you right over like something in the road. You know I will.'

I stepped up to the grille of the Taurus. I laid both hands flat on the hood and put my weight on them, leaning toward Anna behind the windshield, with the deputy, to my right, holding on her steady as a rock, her finger on her trigger.

'Mrs. St. Clair? Anna?' I said, 'You're right. Terry's done nothing. He's in no trouble. You're in no trouble. Yet. But you see where this can go. Please don't let it. Please at least take your vehicle out of gear.' 'So you can come arrest him,' Anna said.

'Uh, Mom?' Terry said beside her.

'I'm not here to arrest anybody,' I said. 'I ask you again to take your vehicle out of gear. That's all I'm asking. What do you say?'

'Mom?' Terry said again.

Anna didn't answer, but she shifted the Taurus into Park and took her foot off the brake. At that, I pushed myself up from her hood and took a couple of steps backward, my hands again raised high.

'Thank you, Anna,' I said.

'Sheriff?' Deputy Gilfeather asked me.

'Mom?' Terry said.

'Stand down, Deputy,' I said. 'Everything is under control here.'

'It doesn't look under control to me,' the deputy said.

'Stand down,' I said again, and Deputy Gilfeather took her pistol off Anna and held it two-handed before herself, pointing toward the ground.

'All the way down, Deputy,' I said. She set the safety on her pistol, put it in its holster on her belt, and stepped back, fixing on Terry and Anna in the Taurus a look of concentration and readiness that was fit to have peeled the paint off the car's bodywork.

There we were. Truth is, I hadn't really planned our moves after the point we had now reached; but lucky for us all, Stan St. Clair that moment drove into the lane. He parked behind me, left his truck, went to the Taurus, and had a word with Anna and Terry. Anna put the car in reverse and began backing up the lane away from us and toward the house. Stan came over to me.

'What's going on here, Sheriff?' he asked.

'Your wife's getting ready to run me over.'

'Hell, Lucian, she offers to run me over a couple of times a week. Tried once, too, but I was too quick for her. She don't mean nothing. You want to see Terry? You know he's here, you might as well.'

'Maybe another day,' I said. 'When your missus is at work.'

'That might be best,' Stan said.

'Okay,' I said. I turned to start back to my truck.

'Wait a minute,' Deputy Gilfeather said to me. 'Is that it? We just check out and go home? We just leave it here?'

'Looks that way,' I said.

'Might be the best thing,' Stan said again.

***

Later that afternoon when she was going off-shift, Deputy Gilfeather lit into me in my office.

'You could have been killed in that thing today, Sheriff,' the deputy said.

'Not likely,' I said. 'You heard Stan. Anna was overexcited. She gets that way a fair amount. She was coming around.'

'No, she wasn't,' Deputy Gilfeather said. 'It was all going south on you. It was hanging by a hair. Anyway, why take the chance?'

'Not much of a chance,' I said. 'When she took her rig out of gear, I knew she was done.'

'You knew?'

'Well, I was pretty sure.'

'You were pretty sure? That's great, isn't it? She threatens your life, and you're *pretty sure*? And anyway, what about her? She was going to assault you with her automobile.'

I nodded.

'She threatened your life, and you gave her please, and you gave her thank-you, and you did exactly nothing. No follow-through. No consequences. You just broke it off.'

'That's the job,' I said. 'The job ain't about always being sure or never taking a chance. It ain't always about consequences. It's about outcomes. We got a good outcome today.'

'You gave in to her,' Deputy Gilfeather said. 'You let her win.'

'I let us all win,' I said. 'Sometimes giving in does that when nothing else will.'

'Come on, Sheriff,' the deputy said. 'Don't give me that Soft Path shit.'

***

As for Terry, he's around. You could say he's learned his lesson. He's stayed out of trouble. In fact, he's done more: the last couple of years, he's been the custodian at the Cardiff Middle School. Of course, the kids call him Captain Hook, but Terry don't seem to mind. He probably reckons things could be worse for him. He's right about that.

It's the way I told Deputy Gilfeather at the time: you need to look at the outcomes. Terry had a good outcome. A worthless young bonehead, hell-bent, cheats the hangman and learns to fly right. Score one for our side. But don't pat yourself on the back too hard. Don't get too cocky. Because, in the worthless young bonehead department, you're up against a very large field. It's like the pickle barrel in the old-fashioned country stores. It's a big barrel. The brine is deep. As hard as you try, as much as you poke around in the barrel, it's never empty. There's always another pickle.

11

A Grapefruit Spoon

As far as we could tell, Nelson Butterfield, in West Bethany, had gotten drunk and started in beating up his girlfriend, Carla Simpkins, when somebody knocked on the door. Nelson thought it was the neighbours again, or maybe it was us, the law. He told Carla to shut up, and he went to the door. That was the beginning of a bad patch for young Nelson over the next twelve–fourteen hours, until early the following morning, when he was dumped off a passing truck in front of the Valley Clinic, unconscious, and with a fat, dirty bandage over his left eye – or, more exactly, over the nasty-looking place where his left eye had been.

For some reason, nobody bothered to call the sheriff's office about Nelson until after eight the next morning. I went right to the clinic, then, but Nelson had gone. The clinic staff had wanted to keep him for observation, but as soon as their backs were turned, he'd slipped out a rear door. I went on to Nelson's place. Nobody home. So I decided to learn what I could from Carla Simpkins, the girlfriend. I got Deputy Gilfeather on the radio and asked her to join me.

Carla worked at the diner in Galilee. Deputy Gilfeather and I found her there. I brought the deputy along for my interview, hoping to get the sympathetic female point of view on Carla and her story – though by then I was beginning to suspect that the sympathetic female point of view wasn't to be had in any considerable force from Deputy Gilfeather.

Carla Simpkins, the deputy and I sat in an end booth in the diner. Carla was a large, soft, slow-going girl who seemed more puzzled than anything else by our attention. (Nelson Butterfield by contrast, was a speedy, sharp-faced rat of a little fellow: how often you see that, don't you? Small men, big women: the mouse riding the Holstein?) Her story was that Nelson had been shoving her around the way he sometimes liked to do when he was drinking. Carla left the impression Nelson's abuse was nothing she couldn't handle. That day, she didn't have to handle it. The knocking commenced: loud, heavy knocking. Nelson went to the door, and a big, heavy-set fellow wearing a kind of hood with eyeholes cut into it slammed in and put Nelson on the deck, then picked him up by the collar, pulled him to his feet, held him, and set about hitting him with his fists. Nelson went down again, and the stranger kicked him in the face with his boot; it was that kick, Carla thought, that put out Nelson's eye. The man then dragged Nelson out the door and drove away with him, leaving Carla alone.

'What did you do, then?' I asked Carla.

'Went to work.'

'Went to work?'

'I had the dinner shift.'

'That was it? Your boyfriend gets the shit beat out of him, in front of you. He gets half-blinded. Then he gets kidnapped. You go to work? You don't call us?'

'Nelson says when stuff happens, you never call the cops,' Carla told us. 'That's unless somebody's dead. If somebody's dead you can call the cops. I didn't think he was dead. He was bleeding a lot, you know? You don't bleed if you're dead, right?'

'Nobody said anything, while all this was going on?'

'No,' Carla said. 'Well, I mean, the big guy with the mask said, like, "Take that, you *bleep-bleep-bleep*." And Nelson said, kind of, "*Unnnhhh.*" You know?'

Deputy Gilfeather spoke up. 'Have you seen him since the attack?'

'Seen who?' Carla asked.

'Your boyfriend,' the deputy said patiently. 'Have you seen Nelson Butterfield since the attack?'

'Oh,' Carla said. 'Sure. They called in the middle of the night, from the clinic, after I got off shift. So I went there and stayed for a couple of hours. He wanted to go, so I, you know, drove him home.'

'Is Nelson home now?' I asked her.

'Uh, no,' Carla said. 'He took off.'

'Took off? You mean he's left town?'

'I don't know,' Carla said.

'I do,' I told Deputy Gilfeather later, when we'd finished with Carla and were getting ready to leave the inn. 'He's long gone. You don't need two eyes to run.'

'Do you want me to keep checking his place?' the deputy asked.

'No point. Forget him. He's clean gone.'

'Maybe,' the deputy said. 'Maybe not.' She was fired up, and rightly so. She had done well. She had asked the hundred-dollar question: had Carla seen Nelson after the assault on him? She had. She'd been with him at the clinic. She'd driven him home. That meant Nelson had had plenty of time to coach Carla on what to tell us when we showed up to question her.

'Sheriff?' Deputy Gilfeather asked me, 'what chances do you think she's telling the truth on what happened? One guy, hooded, on his own? The beating? The kick to the eye? What odds, do you think?'

'I don't know,' I said. 'What odds do you think?'

'Zero.'

I nodded.

'But, why?' the deputy went on. 'That's the thing. Why lie about it? Why does she lie for a dirtbag like her boyfriend?'

'Because she loves him?' I said.

'Because she's stupid.'

'You wouldn't have lied for Nelson, if it was you, I guess,' I said.

The deputy snorted and shook her head.

'What would you have done?'

'First time he laid a hand on me? First time he thought about laying a hand on me? I'd have shot him,' the deputy said.

That's what I meant about Deputy Gilfeather and the sympathetic female point of view. Maybe sisterhood was not one of the things she did well; maybe she didn't have the gift for it. She had the gift for our work, though. She'd sized up the spot Nelson Butterfield was in right off. Nelson's being set on by a single attacker didn't sit right with Deputy Gilfeather. It didn't sit right because it wasn't right. But Nelson had lied about what had happened to him – or he had gotten his slow-motion girlfriend to lie about it for him. That meant there was something or somebody out there that Nelson feared more than he feared us. Now, if you're an ordinary, peace-loving civilian, you may think that's okay. You may even think it's a good thing. But if you're the law, the way I am, you like the one who's feared to be you. You like to have a monopoly on the fear. If you don't – well, then, suffice to say, things can get tricky.

***

Addison was old friends with the head medical man at the Valley Clinic. They got together every couple of weeks to give their elbows a little extra workout.

'Damndest thing he ever saw, Doc said,' Addison told me.

'What was?'

'The guy who came in with his eye mangled. You remember.'

'Oh, that guy,' I said. 'Yes. He'd had it put out.'

'Not exactly,' Addison said. 'He'd had it cut out.'

'Cut out?'

'Yes,' Addison said. 'The eye was removed, it was amputated, you might say, like a surgeon would have done it. There's a surgeon's instrument for it, Doc said, an *oculotome*, or some such: a special eyeball-remover, don't you know. Basically it's a dessert spoon.'

'Come on,' I said.

'No, really,' Addison said. 'What Doc said: a dessert spoon. Or, I guess, maybe, more like a grapefruit spoon,' Addison went on. 'You know, a spoon with an edge? A blade? You've seen a grapefruit spoon.'

'I wouldn't know,' I said. 'Probably not. I kind of leave spoons and grapefruit and all that end of things to you and Clemmie.'

'Dear Clemmie,' Addison said. 'Yes, Doc said it was the damndest thing, that poor devil. It was a new one on him, he said. Doc doesn't say that very much.'

'No.'

'Speaking of Clemmie, how are you two getting along, these days?'

'Great,' I said.

'Good, good,' Addison said. 'Any thoughts about getting back together? Moving back in up there?'

'I don't guess so,' I said. 'Not without we can shift the stud horse to another stall.'

'Ah. You mean Jake Stout, I suppose.'
'I suppose.'

***

Late the same afternoon that we'd interviewed Carla Simpkins, Deputy Gilfeather radioed from Nelson's place in West Bethany. I'd tried to tell her Nelson was gone away, but she'd never believed it. She had stopped there, on her own time, in case he'd turned up. He had. When the deputy pulled her cruiser up in front of the house, Nelson popped out the door and started running for the woods. His eye was bandaged, but he was stepping out pretty spry. The deputy wanted to know if she should give pursuit.

I told her to let him go. It was getting dark; she'd never find Nelson in the woods. Besides, he wasn't important. We could find him if we needed to. And if we couldn't, if Nelson stayed lost – well, that suited me, too.

12

The Intimidator and the Infield

'Do I intimidate you, Sheriff?' the Chairman was asking me.

I had been invited to attend a meeting of the board of selectmen of the town of Cardiff. Now, it may be hard to believe, but selectmen very seldom invite the sheriff to their meetings for the purpose of telling him how grateful they are for the fine job he's doing. Normally, their aim is to complain about the amount of patrolling, enforcement, and other services the sheriff is providing for their town, which is another way of complaining about the fees they agree to pay for those services. The business is done in a form everybody understands perfectly well. The selectmen moan about their assessments. The sheriff moans about the high cost of gas, insurance, dry cleaning, coffee, handcuffs, ammunition, anything else he can think of. It's agreed circumstances are bad and will only get worse unless decisive steps are taken. The meeting is adjourned, and everything goes on exactly as before. It's a lot like Sunday services. It's by the book, and you know the book. I had expected the present evening to be along the same lines.

Wrong. Stephen Roark, the Chairman, started after me almost before I'd got sat down. Why had I not responded with more energy to the alarming incidence of assaults in our community? Had I forgotten the recent battery of Terry St. Clair? Had I forgotten the even more recent, and more aggravated, battery of Nelson Butterfield? It seemed I had. And what about earlier, similar crimes going back months, years? Had I even been investigating any of these acts, these outrages? If so, what had I to report? If perfectly well not, would I admit to being out of my depth, and wasn't it time for the state police, acting with and for the selectmen, to form an independent joint task force concerned with policing our valley, overcoming the authority of the sheriff's department? Would I support such a task force?

'I would not,' I said.

But, why not, the Chairman demanded? Why not, since I hadn't made any progress, myself? Surely, the recent Butterfield incident had to have been the last straw? Was there no limit to my inaction? Wasn't the safety of the whole community at stake? This wasn't about me, after all. Did I think it was? Did I feel unfairly singled out for criticism? By the selectmen? In particular, by the Chairman? Did I feel attacked, here? Myself? By Chairman Roark?

'Do I intimidate you, Sheriff? Are you intimidated?'

'Terrible intimidated,' I said.

It was at this point that Sally Anthony came riding to my rescue. Sally was the Cardiff selectmen's senior member. She knew the town's business, including its legal and parliamentary business, to the last dot on the last *i*. She knew the game, she knew the players, she knew the rules – and she hated the guts, eyes, and soul of Stephen Roark, whom she regarded as an upstart and a specific, personal threat to her authority. Now Sally put aside her knitting and called for a point of order. The Chairman recognised her – and promptly lost control of his meeting. He might as well have gone home then and there. Sally proceeded to lay down a dense bank of smoke and fog, broad and heavy enough to cover the Cardiff Town Charter (1755); the charter as revised (1860); the revised charter as revised (1930); the Constitution of the State of Vermont (1791); the Constitution of the United States of America (1787); the Declaration of Independence (1776); the Vermont Secretary of State's guide to best practices for public boards; the Gospel According to Saint John; and Roberts's Rules of Order. Nobody had any idea what she was talking about, but nobody dared ignore her, especially as the secretary of the board of selectmen was taking down every word, her pen flying across the pages of her notebook. The secretary was Sally's sister-in-law.

At last it was moved to table the matter of the joint state police task force, along with the whole question of recent criminal activity in town, pending a report to be given by me, the sheriff, at a future time. The question was called, moved, voted, passed. Sally had gotten things so inside-out, upside-down, and turned around that not even the Chairman knew how to proceed against her. He sat at the head of the table, blinking like an owl, looking from one selectman to another, turning red, then purple, then blue.

I was off the hook. The secretary thanked me for attending and advised me I might be on my way. I left the meeting. I wanted to stop on my way out and give Sally Anthony a little kiss on the cheek, but Sally had picked up her knitting again and didn't even glance my way.

***

I was feeling pretty trig. I had come out of the Chair's ambush with my hide still on and all limbs attached. I thought I had little to fear from lesser enemies. And so the next morning, on a sidehill cow pasture in Gilead, I was primed and confident. If you can pass through the fire of small town civic administration, you ain't to be frightened by a giant, savage monster dog.

By rights, the matter wasn't one for the sheriff's department, in the first place. In the small country towns up here, complaints and other issues involving animals go to the town constable. I have always been grateful for that. In my experience, people take, and make, a lot more trouble over their pets (especially their dogs) than they do over their neighbours. Let somebody else sort out the lost dogs, found dogs, stolen dogs, biting dogs, rabid dogs, and the rest.

Not this time, though. This time, farm livestock was concerned, and therefore property. Property brings out the real law. Gilead's constable, Homer Patch, passed the ball to me. He asked me to meet him at the foot of Wolcott's pasture, at the bar-way. We'd have to walk from there.

'Bring your shovel,' Homer said.

'Shovel?'

'It would help. And bring your sidearm.'

'Sidearm?'

'Just for fun,' Homer said. He always loved to make a mystery.

Homer, along with Wingate and Cola Hitchcock, made up what you might call the Old-Timer's Infield in our valley: Homer at first base; Cola, second; Wingate, third. 'Old-Timers' wasn't quite right, I guess, since Cola wasn't that much older than me, but it wasn't far out. The three of them *looked like* an infield, too. Cola was small and quick. Wingate was middle-sized. Homer was a big tall fellow who'd stood six-four or -five before he'd begun to be bent over as he got old. The three of them had known one another all their lives, and they went together, worked together, moved together naturally, without much thinking about it – again, like an infield. (Though an infield's four men, ain't it, not three. Our

96

infield didn't have a shortstop, it looked like. Or maybe I was the shortstop.)

I drove out to Gilead and found Homer at the lower entrance to the pasture. We started up the hill on foot. It took time. Homer's almost as old as Wingate, and he ain't built thin. Plus, he had his deer rifle slung over his shoulder, and he'd brought a shovel for himself, which he used mainly as a walking stick to lean on. Going up the scrubby hill, over the rocks and ledges and around the juniper mats, we had to stop often so Homer could puff.

'Getting too old for this work,' Homer said.

'Why are we armed?' I asked him.

'Comfort,' Homer said. 'You'll see.'

Near the upper end of the pasture we topped a little rise. Ahead maybe fifty yards, the woods began, and between us and the woods line, all in and over a shallow dip in the ground, were what was left of two heifers. They had been torn to pieces. Their heads, legs, dripping red bones and shredded hides, their long, blue and pink ribbons of intestine, their other guts, were flung across an area half the size of a tennis court, and the grass and brush all around were tinted brown from their dried blood. Homer and I stood and looked.

'Different, ain't it?' Homer asked me.

'Who found this?'

'Wolcott's boy. They missed the stock yesterday evening. Boy came up on an ATV in the dark. He couldn't see too well. When he figured out what it was, he didn't wait. Turned right around and motored on home. Smart kid. First thing this morning, Wolcott went up himself. He took a look. Then he went home and called me.'

I looked at the torn heifers. They might almost have been run partway through a wood chipper. 'What kind of a thing does this?' I asked Homer. 'A cat?' Homer was more of a woodsman than I was.

'You mean like a mountain lion?' Homer said. 'Come on. You want a lion, go to the zoo. We've got no lions, and if we did, no cat did this. A cat drags its kill off somewhere and hides it. It don't scatter it. That's a dog. Maybe a bear, but I'm thinking that big old dog of the Ginney's.'

'You mean Calabrese? You mean Don Corleone?'

'That one. Calabrese's place ain't that far, cross lots.'

'One dog did this?'

'Hell, Lucian. I don't know. I wasn't here. I don't think the Ladies' Auxiliary did it, do you?'

'You want us to bury them?'

'I told Wolcott we'd do what we could,' Homer said. 'Cover them over. He won't get a cow to come to pasture up here within a quarter of a mile if we don't.'

'And the guns?' I asked.

'I thought maybe the thing would come back for dessert, we'd get a crack at him. What do you call him?'

'Don Corleone?'

'Get a crack at Don Corleone, maybe, I thought.'

'We at him, or him at us?'

'Well, like I said, comfort.'

We set to gathering and covering the heifers as best we could. Rather, I set to it. Those steep back pastures are tough digging. There ain't more than a scrim of soil on top, then rock ledge. Homer soon ran out of gas. Mainly he sat on the ground and watched while I shovelled.

'Definitely getting too old,' Homer said. Then he said, 'How's the missus, these days?'

'She's fine,' I said.

'I heard she moved out.'

'No. That was me. I moved out.'

'That ain't what I heard.'

'I ain't the cause of what you heard, Constable,' I told him.

'I heard she's going around with Jake Stout.'

'That's correct.'

'Jake's a nice enough young fellow.'

'Clemmie would agree with you, it looks like.'

'Still, it ain't a good thing, is it?' Homer said. 'It ain't fitting.'

'I ain't complaining,' I said.

'We know that,' Homer said. 'But it's a situation, ain't it?'

'I don't know if I'd call it that,' I said.

'I would,' Homer said. 'I know others who would, too. Look: don't it seem as though somebody could have a word with him. With Jake, I mean? About the situation?'

'Based on what?' I asked Homer. 'He ain't broken any law.'

'I didn't say he had. I just said somebody could have a word with him.'

'Somebody?' I asked.

'Somebody,' Homer said.

'A word?'

'A word.'

13

Steep Mountain Follies

The Steep Mountain House was what I guess you call today an assisted living facility, what you used to call an old folks' home. It was in the far western part of the county, in the town of Jordan.

Steep Mountain had some history to it. It had been developed and built in the 1970s as Steep Mountain Alpine Village, a top-chop ski resort: trails, lifts, snow guns, base lodge, bar, restaurant, shops, condos – the whole shot. There was a lot of push behind Steep Mountain in those days, and there was a lot of money behind it. But somehow it never caught on, and ten–fifteen years after it opened, it went bust. A Massachusetts company bought it from the banks, dismantled the lift equipment and sold it for scrap metal, let the trails go back to woods, and turned the base lodge, bar, restaurant, shops and condos into the Steep Mountain House, a planned, specialised facility for what the developers called 'elders'. There are more elders coming along than there are skiers, it looks like. The place did pretty well; though people who remembered its beginnings as a venue for skiing liked to say that, whatever reason they were there for, the people at Steep Mountain had always been going downhill fast.

Our mother, Paul, Clemmie and I drove up to Steep Mountain for a visit on a bright late-summer day. Mom had wanted Clemmie to come along. I wasn't sure how that was going to go, but there was no trouble at all. Everybody remained calm. Clemmie kept the gloves on, and I did the same. She even put her hair up and wore a nice blue dress. She looked all right, I thought. In fact, she looked good. I bet Jake thought so, too.

We parked in one of the visitors' spaces. Half a dozen of the residents were gathered near the doors having a smoke. Four women and two men. They and many others at Steep Mountain were nonstop smokers. By rights, every one of them ought to have been dead for thirty years, and yet here they were, puffing away, their ages adding up to somewhere around five hundred years.

Now the director of Steep Mountain, a tall woman in her forties, came to meet us, flapping her arms to part the cigarette fog.

'Mrs. Wing?' she said to Mom. 'Welcome to Steep Mountain House. I'm Barbara Hooper. I spoke to your son, I think?'

'You spoke to me,' Paul said, and he made the introductions.

'Oh,' Barbara Hooper said when Paul gave her my name. 'Lucian Wing, sure. You're in the police, aren't you?'

'He's county sheriff,' Clemmie said.

'Shall we go on in?' Ms. Hooper said. 'I'm sure you'll find a lot of familiar faces,' she said to our mother.

'I'm sure,' Mom said.

Before we got inside, we had to pass through the smokers. Mom knew them all, and all of them greeted us, except for one tiny woman in a wheelchair who said hello pleasantly enough to Mom and Paul, but fired an evil look at Clemmie and turned her face away. I didn't know what was going on there, but then it came to me: the old woman was Clarissa Stout, Jake's grandma. 'Hello, Sheriff,' she said to me, 'nice to see you,' landing on the *you* with just a little extra. Some side-picking had been going on.

We went on into the building, Clemmie and I in the rear. 'The old dragon,' Clemmie said under her breath. 'Tell her to go fuck herself.'

'You tell her,' I said.

'The old bat,' Clemmie whispered.

Barbara Hooper took us over the place in a kind of stroll, going here and there, never in a hurry, stopping often. We saw the common room, the TV room, the bingo room, the fitness room, the crafts room, the dining room. We looked into the kitchen, the laundry, the library, the business and administrative offices. We went up and down the two main halls and inspected the residents' quarters, bedrooms bright and cheerful enough, and not cramped, exactly, but somehow unreal, somehow like children's rooms, like rooms in a dollhouse, thought out according to the ideas, not of the occupants, but of somebody else.

In many rooms we stopped to chat with whoever's it was. There were something like fifty people living at Steep Mountain at the time, and we had a look at all of them, they at us. Paul and Clemmie and I knew a number of the residents, of course, or anyway we knew their names. We knew their children and grandchildren. Our mother must have known all but a couple.

We stopped at Martha Pennypacker's room. Martha had been a schoolteacher at the same time our mother was teaching, but she stuck to it. Now she was retired, her husband had died, and she'd sold their place and moved to Steep Mountain. Now she read and reread the library's books, played bingo, and listened to the public radio stations. To keep her mind active, she did crossword puzzles. Martha did six or eight different puzzles a day – tough ones, nothing from your weekly shopper. It worked. She got the benefit; at least, as our mother said, although Martha might not know for sure who she was or what planet she was on, she could by Jesus do a crossword puzzle.

The climax of our tour, of any tour of Steep Mountain, was the facility's celebrity. Hugh Temple was one hundred and ten, the oldest person in the state and one of the oldest men in the country at the time. He had the best quarters in the place, in fact a suite with a little porch where he could sit and get the sun. Every year on Hugh's birthday, a reporter and a photographer showed up at Steep Mountain to write an article on him for the newspaper in Brattleboro. You would think that, set up like that, Hugh would be a happy old fellow. Not so. He was crabby and temperamental, always had been.

My favourite recollection of Hugh Temple was of the day, now years back, when, already an old man, he had visited our high school history class. Hugh held forth about schooling when he was young, and he made it clear that, in his opinion, things had gone to hell. Schools don't teach you nothing today, Hugh told us students, and he would prove it right here and now. Let's see how much history you kids know, he said. If I'm eighty-six years old today, who were president and vice president of the United States when I was born? Hugh sat back in his chair looking pretty smug, but not for long, because right off little Billy Chambers pipes up, 'William McKinley and Zero.'

'Oh, is that right?' Hugh said.

'That's right,' said Billy.

'Well, then, what do you mean, Zero?'

'McKinley's vice president died. There was no vice president in 1900. Then it was Theodore Roosevelt.'

'Oh, is that right?' Hugh said again. He didn't much like this kid. Smartass little shit. He stomped out of the classroom and never visited school again.

To be sure, since then, Hugh has mellowed out some. He's drawn in. It looks like maybe he ain't going to live forever, after all. He didn't have much to say to us on our visit, or much to add to the occasion, except to reach a dry, spotted old hand out and give Clemmie a friendly pat on the bottom. Well, what if he did? Say what you want, a hundred and ten is no joke. Hugh did pretty well. He ate like a timber wolf, had a drink whenever he could get one, smoked like a brushfire, grabbed every female behind that wandered within range, and was generally said to be as sharp as a tack. Of course, just like with Martha Pennypacker, there's sharp, and then there's sharp. There's tacks, and then there's tacks.

We'd been on our tour for more than an hour when our mother took hold of my elbow and muttered, 'Get me out of here.' Fortunately, we were about done with our visit. We said goodbye to Barbara Hooper and the other Steep Mountain people, and we started for Paul's car. Paul was happy. He was well pleased with what we'd seen. He was all full of Steep Mountain: how cheerful and bright it was, how clean, how well managed and equipped. How nice everybody was.

'What do you, own stock in the place?' our mother asked him.

That stung Paul a little. 'I just liked it, that's all,' he said.

'Great,' Mom said. 'You can move in, then.'

Paul sighed. 'All right,' he said. 'What's the matter with it?'

Our mother was silent. We were taking her home. Paul drove, with Mom beside him in front, Clemmie and I in back, each of us looking carefully out his own window.

'What's the matter with it?' Paul asked our mother again. 'Why didn't you like it? It's full of people you know, people who know you. It's full of your friends.'

'There you go,' Mom said.

'Oh, for god's sake,' Paul said. 'So, you're saying you're not interested in coming here, ever, not even in looking into it more? It's out of the question?'

'Out of the question,' Mom said.

Paul fired his last cartridge. 'You can't just move in, you know,' he told her. 'There's quite a waiting list.'

'Let them wait,' Mom said.

'No, no,' Paul said. 'It's not them waiting. It's you. You're on the waiting list.'

Our mother smiled slightly and shook her head. She might have glanced quickly back at me. She patted Paul's leg. 'I know, dear,' she said.

'Oh, hell,' Paul said. 'If you were never going to even think about moving in there, why are we here now? Why did we – why did you come along today?'

'I wanted to see if it would shut you up,' Mom said.

***

You have heard the one about the fellow in financial difficulties who's asked how he happened to bust. 'How did I go bankrupt?' he said. 'I'll tell you. Two ways: First slowly, then quickly.'

It works for losing your marbles, too, we learned that summer into the fall, thanks to our mother. For some weeks, she would go along on an even keel, and we'd quit watching her, quit worrying. Then she would bump down off the tracks.

When that happened, it was usually Clemmie who saw it first. One day, for example, she stopped at our mother's and, before she went into the house, she could hear Mom, apparently by herself, talking in a loud voice. Clemmie thought she was on the phone. 'I don't know what they're thinking,' our mother was saying. 'They won't have a dog or a cat, but they've got that enormous horse. It just stands there, the horse.' Clemmie went into the kitchen, where the phone was. No Mom. She finally found her on the stairs, sitting on the stairs, halfway up. 'Hello?' Clemmie said. 'Is somebody here?' 'It's Brad,' our mother said. 'He's getting hard of hearing. You practically have to shout at him. Won't get a hearing aid, of course. Silly man.'

Another time, I was in the office doing the end-of-day paperwork when Paul walked in and shut the door behind him. Paul never came to the office. He stepped up to my desk.

'She didn't know who I was,' he said. 'Wendy made brownies for her, and I brought them by. I went in. She was in the kitchen. I gave her the brownies. She was perfectly nice, thanked me, but I could tell: she had no idea who I was. No idea. None.'

Paul began shaking his head. He looked down at the floor. He made a little coughing sound. He couldn't speak. I got up and went around the desk to him. I put a hand on Paul's shoulder, but he shook me off, turned, and went out the door.

I let him go. I thought of going on out to our mother's, but I didn't. For what? To find out if she would know me when she hadn't known Paul? To find out if she wouldn't? Neither was a question I wanted an answer to – either answer. The answer I wanted, we all wanted, was what in the world to do. None of us knew. None of us had that answer.

Then, easily, smoothly, we did. The answer was there. It came flying in over the left field fence like a pigeon, like a homerun in reverse. It came from Addison. I'd been at his place, telling him about our mother, the fix she was in, the fix we were all in. She wouldn't go to Paul, she couldn't go to me, she wouldn't have anything to do with Steep Mountain. We're in a spot.

'What spot?' Addison asked me. 'You're not in any spot.'

'Easy for you to say. What would you do, then?'

Addison shrugged. 'What's the problem?' he asked. 'Bring her here.'

14
The Situation

Lieutenant Farrabaugh called. He wanted to meet. Could I drive up there?

'I guess so,' I said. 'Lunch on you?'

'Absolutely,' Dwight said.

'Usual place? Burger Corral in White River?'

'No,' Dwight said. 'Let's bust loose. Let's go over the water. Burger Corral, Hanover. My party.'

'Hanover? What's wrong?'

'Just get there,' Dwight said.

Hanover is a good-looking town, but it ain't a normal town. It has something supernatural about it, or anyway something foreign, as though it had been dropped complete in one piece from a flying saucer on the hayfields, pastures, and pine woods of middle New Hampshire. With its fine old red-brick college, it has weight, style, class, and a bankroll that don't belong in the place where it's at. Addison will tell you the same thing. He says he always feels, when he crosses the bridge from Vermont, that he ought to be ready to show his passport. And Addison's no stranger in Hanover. He spent four years at Dartmouth – though he claims not to remember much about them.

'Why don't you?' I asked him once.

'I've asked myself that,' Addison said. 'Alcohol may have been involved.'

New Hampshire is where Vermont people go when they want to be invisible. If Lieutenant Farrabaugh needed to meet in Hanover, then something was up. It could only be one thing, pretty much.

I found Dwight out of uniform and sitting at a picnic table off to the side of Burger Corral. He had two coffees, one of which he shoved toward me.

'Are we eating?' I asked him.

'In a minute,' Dwight said. 'Sit down.'

I sat. I took the top off my coffee. It was cold. Dwight had been waiting awhile.

'I wanted to be sure we'd be alone,' he told me.

'Are we?'

'I hope so,' Dwight said. 'Lucian, who the hell is Stephen Roark?'

'The Chairman? Oh, a local bigshot we've got down in Cardiff. New in town. Chairman of the selectmen. A sprinter, you know?'

'What is he in real life?'

'Retired military. Air Force. Had a job in Washington, in the Pentagon. Legal department, or some such. He's a lawyer.'

'Retired, you say?'

'That's right.'

'Christ,' Dwight said. 'If he can fling as much shit as he's flinging when he's retired, I'm glad I didn't know him when he was on active duty.'

'What do you mean? He's a pissant selectman in a pissant town. He can make my life miserable, but he can't do much to you.'

'He can't, but his friends can. He's got hell's own amount of friends, Mr. Roark has. Did you know that? I've heard from my troop commander, from the state's attorney's office, from the fucking governor's office, if you can believe it – three times yesterday. I fully expect when I get back to barracks, I'll have heard from the President and the Secretary of State and the Queen of England.'

'What's it got to do with me?'

'You know damned well, Lucian. This is right along of that little creep Terry St. Clair back then, isn't it? I knew you were feeling weight from somebody when we talked about this the last time. That was Roark, wasn't it? Doesn't matter: it's Roark now. He's after you. He wants to drink your blood. He's telling everybody you're running as a kind of Lone Ranger down there. You're judge, jury, and executioner. Trials? Sentimental nonsense, says Roark says you. You go around punishing suspected troublemakers. Suspected by you, nobody else. You beat them up – hell, beating them up is the least of it. Chopping them up, more like, maiming them. Jesus Christ. Did one guy really lose an eye?'

'Said it happened in a fight.'

'So?'

'So what?' I asked Dwight. 'You mean is it true? I wish it was. I wish I could do that, go around mopping up the scum on my own hook. I have a new deputy who would love to do that, at least she says she would. I told her, forget it, as long as she's my deputy. I'm old-fashioned, I guess. I always thought law enforcement was supposed to be partly about law and not all about enforcement. You know?'

'Okay,' Dwight said. 'But make no mistake. Roark – that is, Roark's friends – are serious. They're getting busy. They're demanding an independent commission to investigate your activities as sheriff. They're talking about a joint task force. God, how I hate a fucking task force.'

'I thought they might,' I said. 'Will they get it?'

'Sure, they will,' Dwight said. 'That's why we're here. I can hold them up for a week, maybe two. But I can't stop them. I thought you ought to know. You have a problem, man. Roark has you locked-in and lit-up. I'm surprised you don't glow in the dark.'

Dwight got to his feet. He nodded toward the Burger World.

'Well,' he said. 'That's today's news. Lunch?'

***

After Dwight had left me to go back to his barracks, I put in a call to Cola's shop in Dead River. I told him we needed to get together. I told him why, or some of why.

'Okay,' Cola said. 'I'll get the others. When?'

'I can be at the shop in an hour and a half,' I said.

'No,' Cola said. 'Come on up to camp.'

I got to Mount Nebo about five to find three trucks parked. Three. I went on over the footpath to the camp. No sign of anybody, but the wheelbarrow was standing near the door, and the door was open, so I went on in.

Sitting around the table, talking quietly, were Cola, Homer Patch, and Wingate. Wingate had trouble with his knees. He could hardly walk. If he'd gotten himself up here, I thought, then they must mean business.

'Look, fellows,' Cola said when I joined them. 'It's the Sheriff of Cochise.'

'What's that?' Wingate asked him.

'Old movie,' Cola said.

'It wasn't either a movie,' Homer said. 'It was on TV.'

'Then how come I saw it in the movie theatre in Brattleboro?' Cola asked him.

'Because you didn't,' Homer said.

'The hell I didn't,' Cola said.

'Fellows?' Wingate said.

Cola dropped it. 'You want a drink?' he asked me. 'A beer? We brought cold.'

'Nothing,' I said.

'Anybody?' Cola asked.

'I'll have a beer,' Homer said.

'I'll have a drink,' Wingate said.

Cola stood up from the table and turned to the sink. 'Two beers and a bump for the old-timer,' he said. He brought back to the table two cans of Bally's Ale, a bottle of Jim Beam, and a glass that he set down before Wingate after blowing the dust out of it and wiping it clean with his shirttail. He took his seat.

'We've got us a little bit of a situation, I guess,' Cola said. He looked at me. 'I told them,' he said.

'What about Farrabaugh?' Homer asked me. 'Where's he?'

'He's safe,' I said. 'He stops with me.'

'You pretty sure on that?' Cola asked me. I nodded.

'What about all these other people, Farrabaugh's boss, the governor's office, all them?' Homer went on. 'Do they stop with you?'

'For now,' I said.

'And later?' Cola asked.

'Depends on the situation,' I said.

'The situation,' Homer said.

'How about Terry? How about Nelson?' Cola asked.

'Terry's around,' I said. 'Solid citizen. Another couple of months, he'll be in the Young Republicans. Nelson? Not seen. By anybody. I'm guessing Nelson's moved on.'

'Good,' Homer said. 'They took the course, then.'

'They saw the light,' Cola said.

'They've been educated,' Homer said.

'Rehabilitated,' Cola said.

'It looks that way,' I said.

'Well, then, that's good,' Cola said. 'Ain't it? That means we've got a situation, but it's one situation. It ain't, like, a bunch.'

'Only one,' Homer said.

'What, then?' Cola asked.

'Well,' Homer said. 'There ain't a lot of choices. It's pretty simple, ain't it? What this situation is is a stick-up nail. You need to do something about it, because it can trip your foot. It can hurt you. So, what do you do? Well, you can try to pull it out.'

'But that don't always work,' Cola said.

'Or, you can bang it all the way back down,' Homer said.

'But that's kind of lazy, ain't it?' Cola said. 'Kind of careless? And then, nail just works itself up again.'

'That's right,' Homer said. 'So, best thing is…' He turned to Wingate.

'Cut it off,' Wingate said. They were almost the first words he'd spoken since ordering his drink. Now the three of them were looking at me, the way I knew, had known, they would be.

'Lucian?' Wingate said.

I nodded.

'Say okay,' Cola said.

'Okay,' I said.

'Okay,' Cola said.

'Dark in here, ain't it?' Homer said.

Cola got to his feet and fetched an old kerosene lantern that he set down on the table, and lit. The yellow light spread over the table like warm honey.

'But, look here,' Cola went on. He spoke to the other two, looking at me. 'This young fellow's taking the job. He's doing the work. On the situation. For us. He's going through for us. Not only that, he's the one with his finger in the dike. He's got his end covered. What about our end? What can we do for him? What does he need?'

'Nothing,' I said. 'There's nothing.'

'Oh, come on, Sheriff,' Cola said. 'You're too modest. We ain't the only ones with a situation, are we? You've got one of your own, don't you? At home?'

'Talking about sleeping in the office?' Homer said.

'Talking about the wife's new roommate?' Cola said.

'We could help you, there. Like I said the other day. Have a word,' Homer said. 'Explain things.'

'Put our case,' Cola said.

'Nothing too heavy,' Homer said.

'No, no,' Cola said. 'Nothing heavy. Just talking to him. Friendly persuasion.'

'*That* was a movie,' Homer said.

'Say what?' Cola asked him.

'*Friendly Persuasion*,' Homer said. '*Friendly Persuasion* was a 'Gary Cooper movie'. *The Sheriff of Cochise* was on TV.'

'Have it your way,' Cola said. 'What do you say?' he asked me.

'What does it matter?' I asked the three of them. 'You're going to do it anyway, ain't you?'

'You bet,' Cola said. 'Whether you like it or you don't, it's still a situation. Ain't it? Situations – that's our department. That's what we do.' Cola's odd eyes glittered in the lamplight. The blue one was the colour and brightness of that stone, a gem stone – what's that one? Sapphire.

'I always liked Jake,' Wingate said.

We were about done. Cola took the empties to the sink and made ready to leave. Then he and I got Wingate up out of his chair and helped him gimp on his bad knees over to the door. Outside camp, in the little yard, Homer was waiting. He helped Wingate get settled in the rusty old wheelbarrow that stood there ready for him.

'Ready?' Cola asked Wingate, and Wingate said, 'Giddyup.' Then Cola and I took turns rolling Wingate along the footpath back to the log landing and the vehicles. It was getting to evening. Either side of the path, close, the woods were thick and dark. Those woods were full of wild animals and birds: deer, bear, moose, coyotes, turkeys, owls, Don Corleone. There might have been five hundred eyes looking at us as we bumped over the path with Wingate riding easy, rocking and swaying in the barrow. Whatever creatures were hiding out there, what must they have thought these crazy humans were getting up to now, rolling one of themselves along through the woods like he was something in a parade?

At the landing Wingate left the wheelbarrow and made it to his truck on his own. He was all set now. He climbed into the truck and shut the door. He rolled down the window and turned to me.

'Been going to ask,' he said. 'How's your mom doing?'

'Not great. She's had a rough couple of weeks. Clemmie and Paul think she's losing it.'

'I heard that,' Wingate said.

'She might go to Addison's,' I said. Wingate raised his eyebrows.

'Addison's? She's going to Addison's? Is that right? Well, I'll be damned.'

'Why?' I asked him. 'What about it?'

'Oh, nothing, I guess,' Wingate said. 'It just struck me.'

'Time to roll, fellows,' Cola said. The four of us shook hands all around. Wingate started his truck.

'We'll be in touch,' he said.

15
Old Number Five

'Bring her here,' Addison said. *What? What was that?*

I took a quick look at Addison. Had he and Johnny Walker been wrestling harder than usual that morning? It didn't look as though they had. No, Addison was cold sober. Had I heard him right?

'Here?' I asked. 'You mean so she lives here? She lives in this house, with you?'

'I guess we could put her in the woodshed,' Addison said. 'Doesn't seem right, don't you know. What about Old Number Five?'

'What's Old Number Five?'

'You heathen,' Addison said. 'The Fifth Commandment: Honour thy father and thy mother – and so on. Old Number Five.'

'Are you serious, about Mom?'

'I'm always serious,' Addison said.

'She'll never come.'

'Want to bet?'

I would have. How often had I listened to our mother tear Addison all up one side and down the other for being a slicker, a snob, a twit, an over-privileged fool; for his alumni dinners, his bow ties, his rich friends, his accent, his profession – especially for his devotion to Scotland's best-known export.

'Lawyer Jessup doesn't know they can make it faster over there than even he can drink it,' Mom said. 'It's such a small country, he thinks, surely he ought to be able to keep up. He'll find he can't.'

'I know some people think Lawyer Jessup's a good-looking man,' she said. 'They ought to see his liver.'

To hear her talk, she had seen it. Mom talked as if she knew Addison inside and out, had weighed him in the balance years, decades before, had found him wanting then, and had had no reason since to change her view. With our mother, Addison couldn't win. He was a fool on his right, a scoundrel on his left, a rummy at the centre. Addison knew exactly how she felt, too. It didn't seem to matter.

'Can she cook?' he asked me.

'What?'

'Can she cook? Your mother. Lorraine. Well, of course she can. Every woman of that generation around here can cook. Right?'

'She kept Paul and me going,' I said. 'Sure, she can cook. She likes cooking, she says.'

'How about the stairs? Can she manage the stairs? How broken down is she? Am I going to have to carry her up, like Rhett and Scarlett?'

'Who's Rhett and Scarlett?'

'People in a book.'

'Oh,' I said. 'No. She don't have any trouble with stairs. She's strong, even. She ain't crippled, you know. She's cuckoo.'

'She'll be very welcome, then,' Addison said. 'Tell her to come ahead, any time she likes.'

'I don't figure you for this, I have to say,' I told Addison. 'Why?'

'Why, what?'

'Why offer to take Mom in? You know what she thinks of you.'

'I do.'

'Well, then?'

'I'll win her over.'

'I doubt the hell out of it.'

'You'll see,' Addison said. 'But, in any case, look here: I'm not getting any younger. I could use the company. A little talk. A little help with this and that. Oh – which reminds me. I know you say your mother can cook. That's very well, too. She can cook. But can she pour?'

***

Tree down at Clemmie's – I mean, at home. Per usual procedures, she called Addison, he called me. Driveway was blocked, he said. Could I get there today? Ain't the driveway blocked for Jake, too, I wondered? But I shut up: I was the one didn't want Jake fooling around my place, wasn't I? So, fair enough. The tree's on me. The chainsaw was in the shed up there, so was the log chain. All I had to do was get on out to Diamond Mountain.

At the house, I saw Clemmie's Accord but no sign of Jake's truck. That Clemmie should have stayed home when I was expected was a surprise to me at first; but, of course, she was stuck there. A main branch of the big double maple by the driveway had split away, coming down right across the lane. I got the saw and chain out of the shed, brought them back to the down tree, and scoped out the job ahead. Then I gassed the saw, got it started, and set to work.

Using a chainsaw is like having the Devil for an apprentice. He's an excellent helper, none better – until he turns on you.

And turn on you, sooner or later, he does. Chainsaws scare me to death, and I ain't ashamed that they do; and I ain't sorry, either. The graveyards of this state are full of confident operators. With luck, though, chainsaw chickens like me may get to die in bed.

The heavy branch was lying across the lane, its butt end driven into the earth by the force of its fall, its length held off the ground by its upper branches. A partway down tree is the most dangerous item in the woods. It's a kind of natural, self-cocking booby trap. It's dangerous because its weight is distributed and supported unevenly along its length. To cut it into sections, you have to allow for that. If you're cutting through a tree in a section that's supported at one end only, that's free, you can cut straight down and the free wood will fall away. If you cut down through a section supported at both ends, though, the cut closes on your chain as you go, trapping the saw. You're out of business. You ought to have been cutting up from underneath, allowing the cut to open as the weight of the tree bore down. But cutting up means cutting toward yourself, and it means cutting blind. That's where you get the kind of accidents like the one that took an ear off Buddy Carpenter a few years ago – or so Buddy said.

I got done in about an hour and a half. Still had two arms, two legs, ten fingers, ten toes: so, a good day with the chainsaw. I used my truck and the log chain to drag the cut trunk and the heaviest branches out of the lane. Then I knocked off. I was beat, hot, covered in sweat and sawdust. I'd tell Clemmie to get Jake to finish up.

I started back to the house to put the saw and chain in the shed, and here came Clemmie out of the house, trotting to meet me.

'Wait,' she called to me. 'Wait there. I've got something to show you.' I put the saw and chain down and waited for her.

Clemmie led me back down the lane, past where the branch had come down. She stopped and pointed to the ground.

'I found this when I tried to drive out,' Clemmie said. 'I stopped and got out to look at the tree. I happened to look ahead, and I saw this in the mud. It's that dog, isn't it?'

Rain had fallen the night before, and the dirt lane had turned to mud. Crossing the lane, printed freshly in the mud, were three tracks of a dog. No ordinary dog: each footprint was near the size of my open palm.

'It's that cop's dog, right?' Clemmie asked me.

'Thought you didn't believe there was such a dog.'

'Maybe I did, maybe I didn't,' Clemmie said. She stood with her arms clasped around her middle, holding herself, as though she were cold. 'I see what I see,' she said.

'Well,' I said, 'whatever it was, it came through here after the rain and before you found the tracks. So, two–three hours? It's long gone now.'

'I'm keeping Stu inside.'

'I would.'

'But, what am I supposed to do?' Clemmie asked. 'I can't just sit in the house and wait for him – it – to come back.'

'Relax,' I said. 'Get Jake to deal with it. Jake will probably scare it off. That, or fight it down bare handed.'

I waited for the bell, then, but no bell rang. Clemmie only said, 'Huh,' and started back to the house. I picked up the saw and chain and followed her. She waited on the porch while I stowed the tools. 'You might as well come in,' she said. 'Say hi to Stu.' She turned and went into the kitchen. Miz hospitality.

At least Stu was glad to see me. He jumped onto the kitchen table and rubbed himself against me, purring. He tried to hook his claws into my clothes and climb up my front, he let me hold him and carry him into the parlour, where I put him down in my old chair, his favourite. Stu was not going to take kindly to being confined to quarters on account of Don Corleone. Couldn't be helped.

Clemmie stood in the kitchen doorway watching us. 'Look at you,' she said. 'You're filthy.'

'Doing your work for you, out there,' I said. 'I got a little messed up. I'm real sorry about that. It's dirty work. It ain't clean work. You're welcome.' I listened for the bell again, but, 'Do you want to take a shower?' Clemmie asked me. *A shower?* I know I said Clemmie was quick to change gears, but this was fast even for her.

'Um, no,' I said. 'I mean, no thanks. I'm supposed to be working.' I remembered the down branch. 'Listen,' I said, 'get Jake to finish up, okay? Tell him he can use the saw. He can cut it up for firewood.'

Clemmie was still looking at me from the doorway. 'Jake?' she said. 'I haven't seen Jake in a week.'

***

Paul wanted that he and I together should put Addison's offer to our mother. She wasn't doing too well. You would sit with her, and she would be right there with you, and then you'd say something, and – nothing. She wouldn't react. In that half-second, she'd have dropped away. She would be looking out the window or at the wall, with her face fixed, alive but no longer there; she'd have gone deep inside, as if she'd stepped off into herself and locked all the doors and windows behind her, and pulled down all the shades.

She was convinced our father visited her. She talked to him every day, often several times a day. Other days, she talked to other people. That was in some ways more weird. Once Paul was at her place and said they'd chatted on very pleasantly for half an hour, until he understood Mom thought she was talking to President Lyndon B. Johnson.

Doing any business from the real world with her took some judgment, therefore. I mean, you had to watch your time. You had to calculate. You couldn't calculate.

'It's a good solution,' Paul told her. He meant Mom's going to Addison's. The three of us sat in the kitchen.

'Solution to what?' Mom asked him.

'Come on,' Paul said. 'You know to what. To where you're going to go to live – eventually. Not right now, but eventually. Addison's offering a solution to that. It's a generous offer.'

'Fiddlesticks,' Mom said. 'All he wants is a cook and somebody to pass the bottle.'

'He could get those things without taking you on,' I said.

'It's a generous offer,' Paul said again.

Our mother turned to me. 'What do you think?' she asked me.

'Paul's right,' I said. 'And, plus, you don't have a choice.'

'Because you won't let yourself have a choice,' Paul took it up. 'You won't come to Wendy and me. You won't stand for Steep Mountain. You're out of options. Addison's the last one.'

'Aren't you two ashamed?' our mother asked us, well pleased with herself. 'Ganging up on a helpless old woman this way?'

Paul stood. I stood.

'So, we'll tell Addison you'll consider it, at least?' Paul asked her. 'Again, nobody's talking about soon. Eventually.'

(By 'eventually' Paul meant not later than next week. Our mother understood that. We all did.)

'Mom?' Paul asked her.

'Well, I guess so,' Mom said. 'I don't know what Brad's going to say, though.'

Paul was happy to play that game with her. 'Dad?' he said. 'Dad knew Addison. They were friends, weren't they? I mean, they are. They are friends, Dad and Addison. They'll get to see a lot more of each other, with you here. They'll hang out. They'll have a great time together.'

Our mother gave him a narrow look. 'Hang out?' she said.

'Sure,' Paul said. 'Dad and Addison.'

'I thought I was the crazy one here,' Mom said. 'Not you.'

'Never mind,' Paul said. 'Don't worry. Dad won't mind.'

In her chair, our mother looked up from one of us to the other. She gave us a little smile.

'He won't?' she asked us.

16
The Click

I haven't seen Jake in a week, Clemmie had said.

Neither had anybody else, I soon found out. Jake had left town, and he'd left in a hurry. The poor fellow hadn't even stopped to pack his blood pressure pills and his new cowboy hat. Jake was gone.

And if he was gone, that meant Cola and them had been at work, as Cola had said they would be. And if Cola and them had been at work, that meant I would soon have to get working, too. Cola knew the rules. He and Homer and Wingate had picked up my end, it looked like. Now I would have to pick up theirs. First, though, best make sure.

I found Cola's shop in Dead River closed, so I went on up to Mount Nebo, to his camp, got there midafternoon. Cola, Homer, and Wingate were there. Homer had laid out a game of solitaire on the big camp table. He loved any kind of cards. Now he was playing, dealing to himself from the pack. Cola was helping.

'You got a red trey, there,' Cola told Homer.

'I see it,' Homer said.

'You could shift that king line… that one,' Cola said.

'I could.'

'Well, why don't you, then?' Cola asked him.

Homer laid down the pack. 'You want to take over?' he asked Cola.

'I'm just saying,' Cola said.

'No, come on,' Homer said. 'Come on, sit down. Show us how it's done.'

'You go to hell,' Cola said.

'Fellows?' Wingate said.

'I heard Jake Stout left town,' I said.

'I heard the same,' Cola said. 'Funny. He was just up here, a few days back.'

'Last Tuesday,' Homer said.

'It was Wednesday,' Cola said. 'I didn't come up to camp Tuesday.'

'Tuesday,' Homer said.

'Fellows?' Wingate said.

'Anyway,' Cola went on, 'Rip invited Jake to camp. Jake's never been up here before.'

'His father used to come,' Wingate said. 'His father used to come into camp with us. Billy Stout? Sure. He was up here a good deal.'

'Jake was tickled to be asked,' Homer said.

'He was tickled, for a few minutes, anyway,' Cola said.

'Later maybe not so much,' Homer said.

'He was tickled, even though it's a hunting camp,' Cola said, 'and there's nothing to hunt. Nothing's in season now.'

'Well, that's Jake, ain't it?' Homer said. 'Brings his bat to the hockey game.'

'Turkeys starting next week,' Cola said.

'That ain't hunting,' Wingate said. Wingate was old school. The only hunting was deer hunting.

'We all had a round,' Cola said. 'Then we got down to business. Rip laid it out for young Jake. About the situation.'

'So even Jake could understand,' Homer said.

'Told him it was about his carrying on with your missus,' Cola said.

'Told him you didn't like it,' Homer said.

'Told him *we* didn't like it,' Wingate said.

'Told him to knock it off,' Cola said.

'Jake denied everything,' Homer said.

'Told us to mind our own business,' Cola said.

'We told him this *was* our business,' Wingate said.

'Told him he wasn't doing himself any good by giving us a bunch of smoke,' Cola said.

'Told him he needed to quit wasting everybody's time and focus on the situation,' Cola said.

'Focus,' Homer said.

'Then we told him what could happen to him if he didn't do that,' Wingate said.

'Did more than tell him,' Cola said.

'Showed him,' Homer said.

Cola left the table and searched around under one of the bunks. He came out with a battered old leather case, not large, about what you'd have for carrying a flute, say. He brought it to the table.

'Gramps's old steer machine,' Cola said. He opened the case. In it, on a worn velvet lining, was what at first looked like a fancy pair of pliers or tongs that you might find in a blacksmith's shop, with the jaws set to come together just at the end of the tool, surrounding a forged opening. The thing was made of bright, highly polished steel. A brass plate on the inside lid of the case read

QUACKENBUSH EMASCULATING FORCEPS

'The old Quacker,' Wingate said.

Cola's grandfather had been a vet in the valley. Today, if you're a vet up here a lot of your business is with dogs and cats, one and another kind of rodent, rabbits, ferrets, turtles, birds, llamas – I don't know what; but in Cola's grandfather's time, the old farming days, a vet was mainly a horse- and cow doctor. The Quackenbush instrument was for castrating bull calves. Cola said his grandfather called it the steermaker or the steer machine, or just the Quacker. To work it, you positioned the tool and clamped its jaws down on the arteries that got blood to the bull's testicles. With their blood supply shut off, the testicles soon shrivelled up and disappeared. No cutting, no injury, no risk of infection. And plus, the steer machine was supposed to be painless, though I ain't sure the bull calves believed that, and I'm willing to bet Jake didn't believe it, either, as he studied the tool where it lay on the table at Cola's camp.

Right off, looking at the Quackenbush forceps, you saw it as a pretty slick, pretty clever little device. You admired it – until you thought about what it did. Then you wanted to cross your legs tight and think about something else. I reached out and shut the lid of the case.

'Are you fellows telling me you've neutered Jake?' I asked.

'God, no,' Homer said.

'We wouldn't,' Cola said.

'Jake might not have been entirely sure about that, though,' Wingate said.

'What did you do to him, then?' I asked.

'Nothing,' Homer said.

'Nothing, much,' Cola said.

'We showed him the steer machine, like we told you,' Homer said.

'Put it to him as one solution to the situation we'd been discussing,' Wingate said.

'The situation of Jake and your old lady,' Homer said.

'Jake agreed that that was one solution,' Cola said.

'By this time, he wasn't tickled to be here so much,' Homer said.

'But he was focusing pretty good,' Cola said.

'We had his attention,' Homer said.

'He still might not have been sure we'd go ahead, though,' Cola said.

'With the Quacker,' Homer said.

'So we showed him the other thing,' Cola said.

'What other thing?' I asked.

'Over there,' Wingate nodded toward the camp's sink. I looked. I didn't get it. 'What?' I asked.

'The window,' Wingate said.

'Take a look,' Cola said.

I went to the sink. Over it was a window, and on the windowsill was a glass tumbler full of a cloudy liquid and with an object floating in it: a white, round ball like a ping pong ball, or a golf ball – or, say, a pickled, peeled hardboiled egg.

'What is it?' I asked.

'Turn it around,' Wingate said.

I turned the glass around so I could see the other side of the egg. It wasn't an egg. It wasn't a ping pong ball. It wasn't a golf ball.

'Jeesum,' I said.

'That's right,' Wingate said. 'Read your Scripture: "If thy right eye offends thee, pluck it out."'

'Is this Nelson's?' I asked them.

'What Jake asked,' Cola said.

'Whose did he think it was?' Homer said.

'By now, Jake's sure of us,' Cola said. 'Jake's a believer, now.'

'And focused,' Homer said.

'Then,' Wingate said, 'we advised Jake that, although the steer machine was one solution to the problem we'd been discussing, it needn't be the only solution.'

'Jake was glad to hear that,' Homer said.

'He was interested,' Cola said.

'He was… He was ready to hear more,' Cola said. 'What's the word?'

'Receptive,' Wingate said.

'Jake was receptive,' Cola said.

'Upshot was,' Wingate said, 'Jake decided to go on his travels. See the country.'

'Seek his fortune,' Homer said.

'And, by good luck,' Cola said, 'we were able to offer him a plan.'

'Call it a work package,' Homer said.

'Jake's in Florida,' Cola said.

'He's working for my cousin, down there,' Cola said.

'Fixing boats,' Homer said.

'Do the boats Jake's working on have to float?' I asked.

'Ha,' said Wingate. 'Good question, but not our concern.'

'Left in a terrible hurry, didn't he?' I asked.

'Terrible,' Homer said.

'You know, that steer machine?' Cola said. 'It makes a little click when you clamp it down and lock it on, there.'

'Just a little *click*,' Homer said.

'We mentioned that to Jake, too,' Cola said.

'Cola's cousin said Jake made it all the way to West Palm in nineteen hours flat,' Homer said.

'New record, there,' Homer said. 'Didn't even stop to piss.'

'Used a milk bottle,' Cola said. 'Didn't even pull over.'

'We did spot him a hundred for gas and food and so on, get him south,' Wingate said.

'I'll take that,' I said. 'It's only right.'

'Decent of you to see it that way,' Homer said.

'I don't have a hundred on me,' I said. 'I'm good for it.'

'We know you are,' Wingate said.

'Take care of that thing of Nelson's, though,' I said. 'Okay? That don't need to be around here. That's disgusting.'

'All in good time,' Wingate said. 'We will, you bet. We'll get rid of it. Count on us. Talking of getting rid of things, though, you've got some getting-rid-of to do, too, don't you? Not that we're hurrying you.'

'Ask you a question?' I said.

'Sure,' Cola said.

'Have you ever used that thing on somebody? That Quacker tool?'

'Ever?' Cola asked me. 'You mean in all the years of coming up into camp, here?'

'Have you ever actually done it?'

'In all the years of camp?' Cola said. 'I don't know about all the years. I haven't been around that long. Ask Rip.'

'In all the years we've been doing this up here, taking care of situations?' Wingate said. 'Well, now, that's a good many years.'

'That Prescott kid,' Homer said. 'We did him.'

'No, we didn't either,' Cola said. 'We didn't have to. He saw the light, just like Jake.'

'He heard the click,' Homer said. 'Then he saw the light.'

'Wrong,' Cola said.

'You just said you don't remember,' Homer said to him. 'You're too young. You said it yourself.'

'I remember Andy Prescott,' Cola said. 'He got the machine.'

'I'm telling you he didn't,' Homer said.

'Fellows?' Wingate said.

17
The Deal-Breaker
and the Pass

Deputy Gilfeather was patrolling in West Cardiff, pretty far out in the brushwood, when she came on our mother walking along the roadside in her bathrobe and slippers. The deputy pulled over, asked if everything was okay. Mom said of course everything was okay; she was on her way to work. Deputy Gilfeather asked her where she worked, and our mother told her at DeJonges'. That didn't mean anything to the deputy. It had been thirty-plus years since Mom had worked for Mr. and Mrs. DeJonge, at their inn, which by now had been closed for probably half that time. The deputy established that Mom had no identification, no money, no keys or other effects. Being new in the valley, Deputy Gilfeather didn't recognise our mother, who refused to give her name. The deputy invited her to get into the cruiser and ride to the sheriff's office. With some considerable air of long-suffering, and with a sharp look at the service pistol on the deputy's belt, Mom agreed to go with her.

Now the three of us sat around my desk drinking coffee.

'You thought you were still working for the DeJonges?' I asked Mom.

'The DeJonges? That's ridiculous,' Mom said.

'Yes, it is,' I said. 'But that's what you told the deputy, here.'

'Fiddlesticks,' Mom said. 'I told her nothing of the sort.'

These days, it was as though our mother had her head divided up into four or five separate rooms, or chambers, the way a big old house gets broken up into separate apartments. There was my long-dead father's apartment. There was the apartment belonging to President Johnson and the like of him. There was Dirk and Margit DeJonges' apartment, shared with other people out of the past. And then there was the apartment where the rest of us lived and might be visited from time to time, when it suited Mom. All these rooms had the doors between them locked tight at all times. When our mother was in one room, the others didn't count – didn't exist, maybe. She moved among them on business of her own that you didn't know about.

'I'm sorry not to have known you, back there, Mrs. Wing,' Deputy Gilfeather told Mom. She looked from Mom to me, from me to Mom. 'Though, now I see you both,' she said, 'there is a family resemblance.'

'Nonsense,' Mom said.

'I look more like my father, I've been told,' I said.

'Nonsense,' Mom said. 'You look nothing like your father.'

***

I drove our mother home from the office. She wanted to know about Deputy Gilfeather.

'I liked her,' Mom said. 'She seems like a good, down-to-earth girl. Good manners. Good-looking, too, in a way – I mean, except for her height. She really is much too tall, isn't she?'

'Too tall for what?' I asked her.

'To be attractive. Though I suppose it might not matter, to her. Did you say she was in the Army?'

131

'Marine Corps.'

'Really? I can never get used to that.'

'To what?'

'Girl soldiers,' Mom said. 'Women. Women soldiers. She doesn't look like the type.'

'What type is that?' I asked. Now for some fun.

'Well,' Mom said. 'You know: the soldier type, for a girl. Woman. That type. Is she?'

'I don't know what you mean,' I said.

'Yes, you do,' Mom said. 'You know perfectly well. Is she?'

'Haven't asked her.'

'She's not,' Mom said. 'Or anyway, not completely.'

'Completely?'

'No,' Mom said. 'For one thing, she likes you. I can tell.'

'Is that right? That's based on all your experience in such matters, I guess, right?'

'Fiddlesticks,' our mother said.

At her place, I stopped the cruiser at the kitchen steps, and Mom opened her door and was getting out, when I said, 'Hold it.' She sat back in her seat, propping the partly open door with her right hand. We sat and looked out ahead of us, to our left, to our right – looked anywhere but at each other.

'This thing today?' I said.

'What about it?'

'This thing today is not just another thing.'

Mom nodded.

'It's a bomb.'

Mom nodded again.

'It's a deal-breaker,' I said

Mom was silent.

'You know what Paul's going to say,' I told her.

'I know,' Mom said.

***

'It's the end of the line,' Paul said. 'It has to be. She's got to do something, now. She's got to go someplace.'

We had met at Addison's. Even Wendy, Paul's wife, was there, though she didn't have a lot to say.

'It's only luck she took off wandering on the road this time,' Paul went on. 'Next time she could get out in the woods, get lost. It could be winter. She could die. She can't stay home by herself. That's all there is to it. Suppose she does. What do we do, put a chain on her? Like a leash on a dog?'

'No,' I said.

'Are we going to put one of those things on her, one of those beepers or whatever they are, as though she's a felon? What do you call those?'

'Ankle monitors,' I said. 'No.'

'Well, then, what?' Paul demanded. 'I'm still for Steep Mountain. She liked Steep Mountain.'

'*You* liked Steep Mountain,' Clemmie said. 'She hated it.'

'Well, then, what?' Paul said. 'You tell me.'

'It's on you,' I said. 'She comes to you. You fix up the spare room. It's easy. I'll help you. We'll put a couple of grab-bars in the bathroom. Night lights. Maybe one of those little seats, on a trolley, goes up and down stairs. Nothing to it.'

Paul looked at Wendy. Wendy didn't have a lot to say. Wendy said, 'No.'

'See?' Paul asked me.

Addison set his glass down on the table with a little rap. 'You people are making difficulties here that don't need to be,' he said. 'I've told you: bring her here. Let her stay here. I'll keep track of her.'

'You can't keep track of her all the time,' Paul said. 'How could you?'

'If she's with me, I'll keep track of her,' Addison said.

'Anyway, she won't go to you,' Paul said. 'She's made that clear.'

'Well, no, she ain't,' I said. 'Not really.'

'Not at all,' Clemmie said.

'Doesn't matter,' Addison said. He took a taste of Johnny W. 'Doesn't matter what she wants or doesn't. Remember your gospel, kids,' he said. '"When thou wast young, thou girdest thyself, and walked whither thou wouldest; but when thou shalt be old, thou shalt stretch forth thy hands, and another shall gird thee, and carry thee whither thou wouldst not."'

Addison liked to quote scripture, though I don't suppose he'd seen the inside of a church since he'd married Clemmie's mother, a union that showed you the use of the prayer book ain't always a guarantee of matrimonial success.

'Hear that?' Addison asked us. '"Another shall gird thee," Leave her to me, your mother. I'll gird her. You'll see. I'll gird the hell out of her.'

***

Deputy Gilfeather knocked lightly on the open door to my office. I sat at my desk, under the lamp. It was after nine at night.

'Come on in, Deputy,' I said. 'Why are you still here?'

'Walter's wife locked herself out of the house,' the deputy said. 'He's gone home to let her in. I said I'd cover. He'll be back in a few minutes.'

'Okay,' I said.

Deputy Gilfeather stepped into the office. She closed the door behind her. She said,

'Sheriff?'

'Deputy?'

'Can I have a minute? I don't want to get out of line, here.'

I thought, *Oh, boy*. I said, "Course you can, Deputy. Sit. What's on your mind?'

She went to the chair across the desk and sat primly on its arm.

'I've been thinking about your Mom, the other day,' the deputy said. 'The poor lady, you know?'

'Yes,' I said.

'Is it Alzheimer's she's got?'

'Nobody's called it that. Or, they haven't, yet. She's young for Alzheimer's, I guess. But she's got something.'

'Poor, poor lady,' the deputy said. 'My grandfather, same thing. It takes over the whole family. It changes everything.'

'Yes,' I said.

'It's a very tough one. On her, on you. Very tough.'

'Thank you, Deputy,' I said. 'You're right. It's tough on all of us.'

'Especially on you, though,' Deputy Gilfeather said. 'What with – this and that. I know things at home haven't been so great for you lately.'

'Things at home are fine as long as I ain't there,' I said.

'I'm sorry, Sheriff,' Deputy Gilfeather said. 'I know I'm out of line.'

'Not at all,' I said.

'But I see you in here, night after night, living in your office. Sleeping on the couch.'

'It ain't so bad. Anyway, there ain't much choice. I don't have a bed.'

'I do,' Deputy Gilfeather said.

I blinked. The deputy was looking at me from her perch on the chair. She lifted her left eyebrow a fraction.

'What are you saying, Deputy?'

'You know what.'

'Dep—' I started. I cleared my throat. 'Deputy Gilfeather,' I went on, 'I refer you to the Chapter on Rules, Item twenty-seven, Subsection C of the Manual for Vermont Deputy Sheriffs: no putting the moves on the boss.'

'We both know there's no such manual, Sheriff.'

'We both know if there were, that would be on page one, Deputy.'

There we sat. 'I thought you'd come in here to quit on me,' I told Deputy Gilfeather.

'Never,' the deputy said.

Two things were in my mind. Our mother was right. And I had just been come on to by my own deputy. *And* I had just been come on to by a lance corporal. I know: that's three things.

There was a sharp knock on the door, which opened to admit Walter, the night dispatch. He was grinning and shaking his head.

'Hi, Sheriff,' Walt said. 'Thanks for filling in for me, Livy. Can you believe it? The house wasn't even locked. Betty couldn't get in because she forgot to turn the knob. Can you believe that?'

18

The Tree Stand

Dwight Farrabaugh sat on a bench across the street from the big inn in Hanover and watched the Dartmouth girls frolic in the warm October sun on the broad college green. Clean young faces, clean skin in all colours, clean hair, clean clothes.

'Not bad,' Dwight said. 'Not bad at all. I wish I'd gone to college.'

'Why didn't you?' I asked him.

'Damned if I know,' Dwight said. 'It's possible there was a certain lack of capital at home. You?'

'Never had the interest.'

'What's interest got to do with it?'

'Well, quite a lot, don't it?' I said. 'You're in college, you're having to study all the time, read. Books. You have to hit the books all the time. Four years or whatever it is. Helps if you're interested.'

'Who said anything about hitting the books?' Dwight watched the girls for a minute. There were also boys, also clean, though not as.

'No, not bad at all,' Dwight said. 'Not a bad way to spend your childhood.'

'They're college students,' I said. 'They ain't children.'

'Yes, they are,' Dwight said.

'Think you can take your eyes off them for a second? Tell me why I had to put the flashers on to get up here in such a tearing hurry? It wasn't just so I could help you look at the show, or was it?'

'No, it wasn't.'

'Why, then?'

'You won't like it,' Dwight said.

'I already don't like it. What is it?'

'Your friend Mr. Roark.'

'Chairman Steve?' I said. 'Okay. What about him?'

'I underestimated him.'

I looked at Dwight. 'Uh-oh,' I said.

'Uh-oh, is right,' Dwight shook his head. 'The other day, at the Corral, I said I could hold Roark's dogs off you for a couple of weeks. I couldn't. I can't. I haven't. They're here.'

'What do you mean?'

'Fellow named Vinny Sutton, State Attorney General's office,' Dwight said. 'Vinny's an investigator. He's their top guy. He's a legend. He gets only the toughest cases, and they always convict. Always. Vinny bats a thousand.'

I was silent.

'I thought, you see,' Dwight went on, 'that Roark would get us to put together a team to look into your, ah, circumstances down there. With the worked-over scumbags? Those circumstances?'

'I think I know the circumstances you mean.'

'I never thought Vinny would get brought into something like this,' Dwight said. 'That's Roark. That's his bigshot friends carrying his water, you see. I thought Roark would get his joint task force. I thought different agencies would be in on it, so I'd be able to run them around themselves, get them chasing their tails and wasting time. Eventually they'd fold it up and go away. That won't happen with Vinny. Vinny fucking concentrates.'

'Okay,' I said. 'When will he start?'

'He's started. Fact is, he's mostly finished.'

'Meaning?'

Dwight took a little notebook from his pocket and opened it. He turned some pages.

'Vinny did what any good investigator would do here,' Dwight said. 'He began by re-interviewing everybody you had talked to. Pretty soon, that brought him around to Carla Simpkins, the girlfriend of the guy who had his eye gouged out?'

'Butterfield. Nelson Butterfield.'

'Vinny leaned on Carla pretty hard,' Dwight said. 'He and Roark saw her together. They double-teamed her. It couldn't have taken very long. They asked her to tell them what happened that night. Vinny led. He gave her the impression he thought – he knew – everything she'd told you was bullshit: again, right out of the playbook.'

'What did she tell him?'

'What did she tell you?'

'She said there was just the one beater: a big fellow in his thirties or forties, wearing a hood over his face. Put Nelson down hard right off, roughed him up, kicked him in the face, smashed his eye, then dragged him off into the night. That was her story,' I said.

'That was her story for *you*,' Dwight said. 'She had a different story for Vinny and Roark.'

'What story?'

Dwight peered into his notebook. He looked at me. 'Three guys,' he said. 'Two older, one of them crippled up some, the third younger but not a kid. No hoods. No beating, or anyway not there. Butterfield went with them willingly – well, maybe not willingly, but he didn't fight them.'

'Did she know any of the men?'

'One.'

'And?'

Dwight shut his notebook. 'One of the old guys she thought she knew. He's your dogcatcher, she thought.'

***

I met Cola at the camp, and together we went through the woods to the spot they called the Orchard. I wasn't sure I could have found it on my own. You went along a logging track for a quarter of a mile, bearing east. Then, when you came to an old stone wall on your left, you turned and followed it north for another quarter-mile. When you got to where you were going, you were so far out in the woods, you might as well have been on Neptune. Believe it or not, though, people had lived out here at one time. The stone wall marked an old farm lane. There was a shallow cellar hole with an ash tree a couple of feet thick growing out of it and a dooryard lilac, mostly dead and broken, standing at one corner. And there were six poor, mostly dead apple trees nearby, set out over maybe a quarter-acre, falling to pieces from the weight of their own dying branches, but still able to produce a reliable crop of knobby, worm-eaten apples. Nobody in his right mind would try to choke down an apple from Cola's orchard; they might have been made on a lathe in a wood shop. But of course the local wildlife crowded in to eat them: deer, bear, moose, coyotes, coons, partridges, wild turkey – all came for the apples. They came for the apples, and the hunters came for them. The Orchard was no orchard. It was a kind of deep woods shooting gallery.

Cola, or more likely his father or grandfather, had carefully cut trees and cleared the brush to make good lines of fire to the six apple trees from different places in the surrounding woods. They had also built three high shooting stands. These were simple platforms made out of rough two-by-fours spiked into the trunks and main branches of big old pines and sugar maples around the Orchard. The tree stands were ten–fifteen feet off the ground. You climbed up to them by short lengths of two-by-four nailed ladderwise to the trunks.

Cola didn't own the woods where the Orchard was. Nobody did: it was state land. In season, anybody who knew about it could hunt in there, any time, and they did. Cola counted on that. We counted on it.

'Okay?' Cola asked me.

'I can find it,' I said.

'In the dark?'

'I think so.'

'You think?'

'I can find it,' I said.

'I'll put up a light here for you,' Cola said.

'We're talking about tomorrow?' I asked him.

'Wednesday.'

'Wednesday? This is Monday.'

'Right,' Cola said. 'Rip sees him tomorrow. Tells him if he wants to question Homer? On the Nelson Butterfield assault? Well, Rip tells him, Homer's up at camp, for turkeys. Rip offers to take Roark up there bright-and-early-first-thing Wednesday. Put him and Homer together then.'

'Where's Homer, really?'

'Visiting his daughter upstate. Been there since last week.'

'That's covered?'

'You bet it is,' Cola said. 'Family reunion, up there. Hitchcocks of all ages and sexes crawling all over the place, taking photos, lots of photos, making memories. Sharp, clear memories.'

'Well, then,' I said.

Cola stopped. He nodded ahead of us. 'I thought about here,' he said.

We stood at the foot of a big pine just beyond the farthest of the apple trees. The stand wasn't one of the higher ones, it was about ten feet up, but it was the best thought-out of the three stands. You could sit on a board seat and steady your gun barrel on a kind of railing. The stand was built right against the trunk, back in among the branches, which had been cut and opened out a little to make the firing port line up with the apple tree, maybe fifty feet distant. The branches hid the stand. A deer, a turkey, looking for windfall apples might come right up to you and not see you. They never look up. Why we build tree stands, ain't it?

'Rip drives him up to camp,' Cola said. 'Far as Rip goes. He can't walk any farther. So I meet them here. Where's Homer? Oh, he went ahead up to the Orchard, looking for a bird; I'll show you where. We take off. We get here. I put him into you.'

I nodded.

'We'll come from over there,' Cola pointed toward the cellar hole. 'I'll be in front. I'll be close to him. I'll block him so he can't see ahead. You're up in here, on the stand, out of sight.'

Now Cola pointed to the ground not more than ten feet from the stand.

'Right there,' Cola said. 'I'll hook quick left, out of the way. Right there. You'll be ready.'

I nodded.

Cola grinned. 'Don't forget: that's me in front, right?'

'Right.'

'Don't – hah – jump the gun. Be ready, but not *too* ready, you know?'

I nodded.

Cola was looking at me. 'You got this?' he asked.

'Hope so.'

'Me, too.'

'Chairman's got some kind of hotshot investigator from the state attorney working with him now,' I told Cola. 'What if they both come?'

'Well,' Cola said, 'in that case, I'm damned if I know. But I wouldn't worry. If this fellow is really a big deal from some office upstate, then he'll most likely be home in bed.'

'I kind of wish it could be sooner,' I said. 'Tomorrow. If it's got to be.' But Cola shook his head.

'Can't be helped,' he said. He patted me on the back. 'Bring them up tight,' he said. 'Bring them up tight, and hold them high. You'll be fine. Are you all set for hardware?'

'I don't know,' I said. 'There's the ones in the rack at the office.'

'I wouldn't use any of those, though,' Cola said. 'You never know how they can connect things up. Tell you what: stop by, today, tomorrow, see Rip. He'll fix you up with something.'

I nodded.

'Listen,' Cola said. 'Just don't think about it. Okay? Don't think about it, and don't think about it. Then do it, Right?'

'Right,' I said.

***

Wingate was tickled. 'Oh, sure,' he said, and he hobbled over to his kitchen door. The door was open. Wingate reached behind it and brought out an old Winchester shotgun, a pump-action 12-gauge with a hammer and a short barrel. He brought it to the kitchen table, where he worked the action back and forth with a loud clatter. Five shells popped out and landed on the table.

'Model of eighteen and ninety-seven,' Wingate said. 'The Old Trombone. An American classic. The Model T of buckshot guns.' He sat and regarded the Winchester fondly. 'You ever used one of these?' he asked me.

'Used ones like it,' I said.

'There's nothing like it,' Wingate said. 'Kicks like a mule. God, I remember one time years ago when I was deputy to the old sheriff, Charlie Tavistock. Charlie could be pretty nuts. This was his gun. So, one day, Charlie and I are sitting around his place, and I guess we might have had a couple of beers. And we were looking across the road at Ben Doolittle's field of ripe pumpkins. Well, Charlie never liked Ben. He decides it would be fun to go over there, blow up some of Ben's pumpkins.'

'There's law enforcement setting a fine example for the rest of us, ain't it?' I said. 'The sheriff and his trusted deputy, drunk, disorderly, armed to the teeth, and causing wanton property damage. Good to see.'

'Sure,' Wingate said. 'Well, Charlie goes into the house, fetches this gun right here, and off we go across the road to the pumpkin field. Charlie's loading shells into the gun. He goes up to this big old pumpkin, cocks the Winchester, throws her to his shoulder, and lets her go. Knocked Charlie right over backwards on his ass. Cracked a rib, thought he'd dislocated his shoulder. Charlie wasn't happy. He gave the gun to me.'

'What did it do to the pumpkin?' I asked Wingate.

'Blew it all to shit. Oh, she'll do the job. Depend on it.'

Wingate proceeded to load the shells back into the shotgun. He shoved it across the kitchen table to me. 'Take good care of her,' he said.

'You keep it around loaded?'

'Don't do you much for you if it ain't, does it?'

'What are you worried about, though?'

'Housebreakers. Dope fiends. You know: burglars looking for money for dope.'

'You'd kill a man for that?'

'Sure,' Wingate said. 'Hell, Lucian, anybody who thought it might be worth his while to break in here is too dumb to live, anyway.'

***

Our mother made as if she would move into Addison's house with all her possessions in a single bag. When Paul and I came to pick her up, she was standing in the kitchen with her cardboard suitcase at her side. She looked like somebody who had just stepped off the boat from someplace onto the pier in New York City.

'That's all you're taking?' I asked Mom. 'Come on. This ain't a slumber party, you know.' But Paul shushed me. 'It's fine,' he said. 'Everything's good. Let's go.'

At his house, Addison was waiting out front. He shook hands with our mother.

'Hello, Lorraine,' he said. 'Lorrie. Hello, Lorrie.'

'Hello, Addison,' Mom said.

Addison stepped aside and let her go before him into the house. She went to the stairs and up. We followed. The room that would be hers had been the main bedroom. She went right to it. Addison slept downstairs in a chamber off his study. Closer to the bar, I guess.

We watched our mother go over her room. She looked out the windows, she sat on the bed, she looked into the closet, into the bathroom. She opened the drawers of the big walnut dresser. She turned to us with a grin.

'This knocks the spots off Steep Mountain,' she said.

'It's okay?' Paul asked her. 'You like it?'

'I do,' Mom said. 'I don't know what Brad will say.'

Paul was ready for that one. 'He'll be glad you've got a place of your own,' Paul said.

'A place of my own,' our mother said. 'Yes. He'll like that.'

She lifted her suitcase onto the bed, opened it, and began unpacking it into the dresser. Paul and I looked at each other. The suitcase was full of nightgowns. Nothing but nightgowns. Nightgowns of different colours, different materials, different weights, different styles were all that was in there. Now Mom was taking them out, one by one, smoothing them carefully on the bed, and folding them into the top drawers of the dresser. Nightgown after nightgown after nightgown came out of the suitcase. It was like a magic trick.

'What are all these?' I asked Mom.

'You see what they are,' she said. 'They're nighties.'

'What do you need so many for?' I asked her.

'Mind your own business,' our mother said.

She put away the last nightgown and shut the suitcase. Paul put it in the closet. Our mother looked around the room again. She returned to the window that faced west.

'Look,' she said. 'You can see Mount Nebo.'

'Is that Nebo?' Paul said. 'I guess it is.'

'Brad will like that,' our mother said. 'He goes hunting on Mount Nebo.'

'Sure, he does,' I said. 'At Cola's camp.'

'Cola's camp,' Mom said. 'Brad never had much luck at camp. I did.'

'You were a deer hunter?' Paul asked her. 'I don't recall you were.'

'Before your time,' Mom said. 'I hunted. I liked hunting well enough. But I got my deer. So I quit. Brad never got his deer.'

'Well, they have fun even if they don't have luck,' Paul said. 'Hunters.'

'They do,' Mom said. 'They surely do.' Then she said, 'I think I'll lie down for half an hour.'

We left her. Addison thought we should all have a drink, but I had to get back to the department. Paul drove me.

'Our mother, you know?' I said to Paul. 'That must have been twenty-five or thirty nightgowns. No dresses, no underwear, no toothbrush. What's she thinking?'

'You heard her. It's for Dad. She thinks she needs to look good for Dad. He'll be coming around, she thinks. She wants to be ready for him.'

'Oh.'

'Cuckoo,' Paul said.

'Yes.'

'Wendy's at her place right now,' Paul said. 'She'll pack up and bring the other things. We'll just go get what Mom needs, when she needs it. Easy does it. One day at a time, Little Brother. Okay?'

'Okay.'

'But I still wish she was at Steep Mountain,' Paul said.

'Why?'

'Community. She needs a community. Steep Mountain is that. One cuckoo is only a cuckoo. Fifty of them's a community.'

'This community, anyhow,' I said.

19
Death of the Don

'Don't think about it,' Cola had said. That turned out to be easier than you might have expected. In the circumstances, I mean. Something else came up.

Back at our office after leaving Wingate's, I first locked his old shotgun in the rack, then went out front to see what the dispatcher had in the way of business. Deputy Gilfeather was there. Since our late-night conversation of a couple of days before, the deputy and I hadn't had a lot to say to each other. She was out of the office, or I was. That suited me. I wasn't sure what my line with Deputy Gilfeather ought to be right now. Where were we, exactly?

Don't think it hadn't occurred to me that, strictly as a matter of accounting, I could claim a free pass from Clemmie where the deputy was concerned – more than one, truth be told. Strictly on the book, I mean, I was running a credit balance with Clemmie. On the book, I was. But there ain't no book. And plus, Deputy Gilfeather ain't my type. Mom's right: she's too tall for me.

Also, I still thought the deputy was getting ready to resign. She must know she's wasted up here. She must have figured that out by now. She'll be moving on. But she kept on not doing that.

I was standing at the dispatcher's desk when the phone rang, and here's Clemmie, red-lining, close to hysterical, carrying on and on about the dog, the killer dog, Don Corleone. He was there, at the house, and he had Stu the cat trapped up on the shed roof. As soon as he could figure out how to get up there, the dog would move on Stu. Or Stu would panic and try to make a break for safety by leaving the roof. Either way, he was a goner. Clemmie was afraid to leave the house. She couldn't tell exactly where the dog was; he kept moving around the building. But she had seen him, he was enormous, he was fast, and he was there, right there, with her. On Don Corleone, Clemmie had come around, no question. She began by not believing he existed. Then she wasn't sure. Now it sounded like she was believing in him pretty hard.

'Come on,' Deputy Gilfeather said, and she and I started for the door.

My truck was parked at the corner of our little lot, but the deputy's cruiser was right out front. We took it. The deputy turned on the blue lights, turned on the screamer, and put the hammer down. We flew out of the village and up the road to Diamond Mountain.

We were just turning into our drive when it occurred to me that I had no weapon. I don't carry one, don't allow them to be kept in the cruisers. In our vehicles, most guns are a bother, is all they are. You forget about them. They get dirty and rusty and unreliable. Right now, though, if we were going up against Don Corleone in a few minutes, I wouldn't have minded the bother so much, but too late for that. As for Don Corleone, I'd just have to reason with him.

At the house, seeing nothing in front, the deputy didn't hesitate. The cruiser left the driveway and sped around to the back, over the mowed lawn, skidding and spinning, ripping up grass.

There they were. We had a little lean-to woodshed off the kitchen, and Stu was crouched on its roof, a low roof, but high enough to stop, at least for now, the animal that ranged back and forth on the ground beneath him.

It was a dog, all right, and it was huge: as big as a small pony and with a massive head and forequarters. It had the long, alligator jaws of a shepherd or a wolf and the teeth to go with them, and it had the bulk through the head and shoulders, the hard, solid, muscular power, of a pit bull or mastiff, or some such breed. But what you noticed first about Don Corleone wasn't his size, it was his thinness. He had a starved look, all angles and bones, like a skeleton. He had a brindled coat, grey and black, and the markings made his ribs and backbone look even leaner than they were. He looked like the living, moving X-ray of a dog, and as he wove back and forth in front of the shed, like a prize-fighter who has the other fellow in a corner and is looking for an opening to go in and finish him, he kept his eyes fixed on Stu, up on the roof.

Give him credit, Stu was game. His fur was fluffed out to make him half again as big as he really was, he was hissing and spitting like a cobra, and his eyes blazed with rage and terror as he moved to keep facing the dog. Don Corleone, for his part, made no sound that I ever heard, from the beginning of our business to its end.

When Deputy Gilfeather and I came around in the cruiser, the dog broke and ran for the woods, maybe a hundred feet away. The deputy tried to follow in the cruiser, but she bottomed out on the softer, uneven ground, and her left rear wheel began to spin. End of the road. Deputy Gilfeather stomped on the brakes, and we slewed to a stop. We each threw open his door and took off running after the Don. I was in the lead, unarmed, the deputy was somewhere close behind me.

There's an old stone wall that runs at the rear of our house, about two-thirds of the way between the house and the wood's edge. I had been trying to keep it up: replace the fallen stones and set them back in the wall so they'd stay put. That day, I wished I hadn't been so neat. Rather than being a low pile of tumbled rocks, this particular section of the wall was square, plumb, and four feet high. Don Corleone took it in one long bound, like a fancy horse at a steeplechase. I had to stop and scramble over on my hands and knees. While I was doing that, Deputy Gilfeather caught up with me. She went at the wall like a hurdler, full tilt, not breaking stride, and with one leg thrown out and over. She landed fast and went right on after the dog, with me now following her.

When Don Corleone reached the woods, we were not more than twenty feet behind him. I thought we'd lose him in the trees, then, but no: he stopped in front of a big sugar maple just at the edge of the woods. There, he turned at bay. The Don was all done running. Time to show down.

The deputy and I halted. The dog crouched, it looked like he was about to come right at us. I put my right hand to my belt: nothing there. I remembered: no piece. *Uh-oh*, I thought, but in that half-second, Deputy Gilfeather standing just off my left shoulder, raised her service pistol, braced, and opened fire.

She gave him the whole clip. Her first round went high; we saw it take a piece of bark off the tree behind Don Corleone. But every one of her follow-up shots went home in the dog's left side, forward: heart-shots. The brass cartridge casings that her gun popped out as she fired fell about my head and shoulders like hot rain, and I made to cover my ears, but it was all over in a couple of seconds. Don Corleone's hindquarters failed, he went down, tried to rise, went down again, stayed down.

Cautiously, we approached the dead beast. The deputy was some kind of shot: you could have covered the seven or eight bullet holes in Don Corleone's side with a saucer. She was saying something.

'Say what?' I asked her. She had been firing two feet from my left ear.

'I said, look at the size of him,' Deputy Gilfeather said.

'Can't hear you.'

'Big, I said.'

I nodded. 'That's some pistol shooting, Deputy,' I said.

'Not in the Corps,' the deputy said. 'This range? And the first one a bogie? No badge.'

'Did the trick, though,' I said, looking at the body of Don Corleone.

'Well, yeah,' Deputy Gilfeather said, 'it did.'

***

When the deputy and I got back to the house, we found Clemmie waiting for us on the porch, holding Stu in her arms.

'I heard shots,' Clemmie said. 'Is it dead?'

'Yes,' I said.

'Did you shoot it?' Clemmie asked me.

'Deputy Gilfeather shot it,' I said. I remembered that Clemmie and the deputy had never met. 'Clemmie, this is Deputy Olivia Gilfeather,' I said. 'Deputy, this is Clemmie.'

'Clementine,' Clemmie said. She looked the deputy up and down. Then she said, 'Clementine Wing.' She and the deputy nodded to each other. The deputy didn't say anything.

Clemmie put Stu down on the porch, where he flopped onto his side and made himself comfortable, stretching out in the sun. Stu didn't look like a cat who'd just escaped being eaten alive by a monster dog. *Dog? What dog's that? Did somebody see a dog?* Stu was saying.

'Is it really dead?' Clemmie asked me. 'You're sure?'

'Dead as anything ever gets,' I said. 'The deputy don't miss.'

'What did you do with it?' Clemmie asked.

'We drug him into the woods a little way,' I said. 'Let the coyotes and them take care of him.'

'Couldn't you bury it?' Clemmie asked.

'Not right off,' I said. 'You saw the size of him. He must weigh two hundred. Bury him, you'd need equipment.'

'Then get equipment,' Clemmie said.

'I'll call somebody,' the deputy said. 'When I get back to the office.' She went to the cruiser. 'Do you want a ride back to town, Sheriff?' she asked me.

'I'll take him back,' Clemmie said.

I looked from Clemmie to the deputy, back to Clemmie, back to the deputy.

'I'm going there, anyway,' the deputy said. 'To the office. I'll take him.'

'He's my husband,' Clemmie said. 'I'll take him.'

'Sheriff?' The deputy turned to me.

'I'll be along shortly,' I told her.

'Suit yourself,' Deputy Gilfeather said. She went to the cruiser got in, started up, backed around on the grass, and drove off.

'She's got her eye on you, that one, doesn't she?' Clemmie asked me.

'What?' I said. ''Course not. 'Course she don't. She's my deputy.'

'She'd like to be more,' Clemmie said.

'You've got nothing to worry about from Deputy Gilfeather,' I told Clemmie. 'She's too tall, and plus, I make it a point not to get involved with women who shoot better than I do.'

'Ha, ha, Sheriff,' Clemmie said. Then she said, 'Do you want to come in for a minute?'

'What for?' I asked. 'Is the commode running?'

But Clemmie wouldn't ring the bell. She rolled her eyes. 'I'm asking you, Lucian,' she said. 'I'm asking you to come in. Lord, you saw that thing. I don't want to be alone out here with the woods full of things like that. I'm frightened.'

'Don Corleone was by himself,' I said.

'Do you know that?'

'No. I guess I don't, not for sure.'

'Well, then?' Clemmie said.

'You want protection, you can do better than me. Get the deputy. She's the one put seven out of eight into the bulls-eye on Don Corleone. I couldn't have. I can't shoot like that, never could. You're afraid of the dog? You want defence? Get Deputy Gilfeather.'

'I'd rather have the dog,' Clemmie said. 'Are you coming in, or not?'

Well, it took us a couple of hours, what with one thing and another, but Clemmie and I got things settled between us that afternoon, or on the way to settled. We got to where the fight was over, the gloves were put away, the ring was rolled up, the lights were turned off. After, driving back to town in Clemmie's Accord, we met Al Partridge, an excavator and the night dispatcher's brother-in-law, rocking and grinding and jouncing up the hill in his backhoe, on his way to bury Don Corleone.

20
Recohabitation Day

When I walked in past the dispatcher's window at the department the next morning sharp at seven, Walter, the Prince of Darkness, was going off shift. Seeing me in front of him, he about dropped his teeth.

'What are you doing out here?' Walt asked me.

'I work here, same as you,' I said.

'I know, but what are you doing, *here*? You're not here. You're back there.' He glanced behind him at my office door.

'Not any more.'

'Where, then?'

'Home.'

'Is that right?' Walt asked. 'Took you back in, did she?'

'It looks like she did.'

'We thought she would,' Walt said. 'Well, Livy thought she would. I wasn't so sure. I know you better than Livy does.'

'Thanks,' I said.

'Either way, congratulations, ain't it?' Walt said.

'Thanks again. Glad to be here.'

'You won't be,' Walt said. 'You've got an early customer.'

'I saw his vehicle out front. How long has he been waiting?'

'Long enough.'

In my office, I found the Chairman sitting in the visitor's spot in front of my desk.

'Mr. Roark,' I said.

'Sheriff,' the Chairman said. 'You're punctual, at least.'

'Punch in at seven,' I said, 'just like everybody else.'

I went around the desk and took my chair. I sat. I faced Roark across the desk.

'Do you want a coffee?' I asked him. 'I can get somebody to bring us some. I can bring it myself.'

'No coffee. I'm not here on a social call, Sheriff.'

'Didn't suppose you were.'

'Fact of the matter is, I'm here to apologise to you.'

'Apologise?'

'That's right, Sheriff. I owe you an apology. I pay what I owe.'

'An apology for what?' I asked him.

'Well, that's an odd thing,' Roark said. 'I'm not at liberty to tell you, or not in detail. Not right now. It's confidential, get it?'

'I'm not sure I do.'

'You will,' the Chairman said. 'It will come out in the next day or two. But what I can tell you, what I'm here to tell you, is that I had you wrong. I misjudged you, and for that I apologise.'

'Had me wrong, how?'

'I thought you were behind the attacks,' Roark said. 'Terry St. Clair. Nelson Butterfield. The ones before them. I thought they were your work. I had reason to think so. Those were assaults resulting in grievous bodily harm. They were serious crimes, very serious crimes. But you didn't seem too interested in investigating them. I thought that was because you were guilty of them, yourself. I thought you'd decided you were a secret, one-man court up here, no need of help from the real courts: you'd do it all yourself. You'd become a vigilante, I thought. You wouldn't be the first cop to go feral. That was what I thought.'

'But now you know different,' I said.

'Now I know different.'

'How?'

'Don't you get it, Sheriff? That's what I can't tell you. I'm working with one of the top people from an office in the state capital. Which office, I can't tell you. We've got about ninety percent of the story now. In another day, two at the outside, I'll have the rest. It's quite a story, I can tell you that. Put it this way: I was wrong about you, but I wasn't wrong about everything. Do you know Homer Patch?'

'The Gilead constable? Sure. Is he part of this?'

'Absolutely. The question is: is he all of it? That's what I'll know tomorrow morning, when I've talked to Patch. Do you know the junkyard guy in Dead River? Cola? Cola Hitchcock?'

'Sure.'

'Do you know his deer camp?'

'Yes.'

'Have you been there?'

'Maybe once or twice.'

'Good,' the Chairman said. 'Then you can meet us there tomorrow first thing.'

'Can't do it,' I said. 'I've got something else tomorrow morning.'

'Is it important, Sheriff?'

'I'd say so.'

'It had better be,' the Chairman said. 'My business goes directly to the safety and welfare of this whole community. Get it?'

'So does mine,' I said.

I watched him. He made me curious, now, so I watched him. He was like a man driving a fast car who don't know he's got no brakes. He kept telling me to get it. *Get it?* he said. *Get it?* Wrong. The Chairman was the one who didn't get it. He still thought he was the boss. He still thought he had all the cards. He had nothing, worse than nothing. He didn't know that yet, but I did, and the Chairman would know it soon enough.

Another day, two, the Chair said, he'd have had it all. Well, he wasn't wrong about everything, was he?

'What about your partner from upstate?' I asked the Chairman. 'Will he be at Cola's?'

'No,' Roark said. 'Patch will be there. Hitchcock, too. They wouldn't talk to an outsider.'

'But they will to you?'

'I'm an elected town official, Sheriff,' Roark said. 'They won't have much choice.'

'If you say so.'

'I do say so.'

The Chairman gave me a long look. He shook his head. 'You know, Sheriff,' he said, 'I came here to apologise to you, and I've done it. Apologising doesn't come easily to me. Apologising's not something I enjoy.'

'There's very few do,' I said.

'And now, when you tell me you won't help question Patch and Hitchcock? When you have better things to do? When you don't seem keen or even much interested? Let me be honest with you: I'm not surprised. No, Sheriff, I'm not surprised by your attitude, here. I've seen it before, in you. In fact, I haven't seen much else. Yes, I got you wrong. I thought you were guilty of maiming St. Clair and the others. I was wrong about that, and that's my apology. I thought you were a criminal. You're not a criminal. But I didn't get you all wrong. You may not be a criminal. But you are a lazy, ignorant, irresponsible, incompetent dolt. You're a joke, Sheriff. I've known good men who chose to act the part of the dumb woodchuck because it suited their purposes. I'm guessing your predecessor, Sheriff Wingate, was one of them. I wish you were, too, but you're not. In your case, Sheriff, dumb woodchuck is no act.'

'You want me to show you on the map how to get to Cola's place?' I asked him.

'No need,' the Chairman said. 'I'm driving there with Wingate.'

'Wingate's part of this, too?'

'He is indeed, Sheriff. He's been very helpful. Sheriff Wingate is an impressive man.'

'He sure is.'

'You see, Sheriff, we have this thing surrounded. Get it?'

'Got it,' I said.

***

'Snooper,' Clemmie said.

We were lying there, that second night I stayed at home. Stu the cat was asleep between us. Clemmie, in her nightgown, had her glasses on. She was sitting up with her back against the headboard of the bed and a book on her knees. Clemmie's a reader. She likes mysteries that happen in foreign countries. I don't have a lot of time for reading. When I start in reading something, I get itchy. I lay beside Clemmie, three quarters asleep. At first I thought she was talking about something in her book. 'Mmm?' I said. 'Who's a snooper?'

'You are,' Clemmie said.

I was awake now. As I have reported, it's tough to stay ahead of Clemmie. She moves fast. Even when she breaks training, like now, she keeps her footwork sharp.

'What are you talking about?' I asked her.

'I knew you'd come around spying and snooping. I knew you couldn't resist doing that. That day in the woods?'

'What day in the woods?'

'You know perfectly well what day. The day Jake and I were up there. I heard somebody sneaking toward us, spying on us. That was you.'

'The hell it was,' I said.

'And then when you came to fix the window,' Clemmie went on. 'You were snooping around in my dresser drawers, weren't you?'

'Absolutely not,' I said. 'What gave you that idea?'

'I can tell,' Clemmie said. 'I can tell right now. You're a lousy liar, Sheriff.'

'Not like you and Jake, you mean,' I said.

'Ha, ha,' Clemmie said.

'You're right,' I said. 'It ain't you *and* Jake who's the liars. Jake ain't got the smarts to lie.'

'Don't be too hard on poor Jake,' Clemmie said. 'He's okay. Jake goes where you point him.'

'That he does.'

'Did you know he's moved to Florida, Jake?' Clemmie asked me.

'Is that right?' I said.

'That's right,' Clemmie said. 'So here we are.'

'Until the next Jake comes along.'

'Maybe there won't be a next Jake,' Clemmie said.

'But if there is?'

Clemmie put her book on her bedside table. She turned off the light on the same table. She slipped down beside me under the covers and stretched. She patted my knee. 'Let's play that one by ear, shall we, Sheriff?' she asked me. She turned on her side and prepared herself for sleep.

'Whose ear?' I asked.

***

'Clemmie tells me you're back,' Addison said.

'I would have said it was Clemmie who's back,' I said.

'Either way, it's good news,' Addison said. 'Didn't I tell you she'd come around?'

'You did.'

'What happened to her, ah, friend?'

'Trying a warmer climate.'

'Sound move. I couldn't be more pleased, though, about you two. You belong together. Not that it's always smooth.'

'No, it ain't,' I said.

'You know our girl,' Addison said. 'She's restless. She's strong-willed. But she's faithful in her way. A lass unparalleled, Lucian.'

'Unparalleled,' I said.

'I have to tell you, though,' Addison went on. 'She's not best pleased about Calamity Jane. Your new deputy. She's jealous, don't you know. It's only fair, I suppose. You were jealous. Now it's Clemmie's turn.'

'I wasn't either jealous.'

'Of course not. Of course you weren't.'

'Jealous of Jake? Ha.'

'Of course,' said Addison.

'Anyway,' I said, 'she don't have to be pleased about Deputy Gilfeather. I do. I don't need a wife. I've got one. I do need a deputy. A deputy's what I've got. It's all she is.'

'Of course,' Addison said again. 'Of course. But, really, this is a big day. It ought to be a holiday. Recohabitation Day.'

'Say what?'

'Recohabitation Day. Getting-Back-Together-Again-Day. How about it?' Addison said. 'We'll celebrate. I'll take us out to dinner. Maybe a few drinks. Lorraine, too. How about tonight?'

'Not tonight.'

'Why not?'

'Can't. I'm going out of town. Be gone overnight.'

'Ah,' Addison said. 'Sheriff's business, I expect?'

'I expect,' I said.

161

21
The Orchard

In the end, this is how we worked it. Tuesday noon, I told the dispatcher I'd be gone for the day. I drove my truck, didn't take one of the cruisers. First thing, I got the river road and stopped for gas at the store on Route 10. I paid with the sheriff's department's card, bought a cup of coffee, and chatted with Suzanne, who had the counter.

What do you think happened when I got ready to leave? I spilled my coffee all over the counter, all over Suzanne, all over myself. Clumsy me. We cleaned it up, and Suzanne gave me a fresh cup free for nothing.

Then I drove on to Bethany, where I stopped at the school. I sat down with the principal there, and we went over a program he wanted to put on with the help of the sheriff's department to get the students to lay off tobacco and beer and dope and sex and things of that nature. We had a late lunch in the school cafeteria, and I went up the road to Galilee, where I found the minister of the church in the village trying to figure out how to hook up the vestry's new TV. Between us, we got it going, and then the minister showed me where somebody had spray-painted some trash all over the stones in the cemetery. He had taken some photos, and he gave them to me, but we both knew there wasn't much chance we'd ever find the vandals. We talked about that. We agreed there's no telling what's going to come next from kids today: kids today get into some bad business. Yes, they do. Goddamned kids.

By now it's past quitting time. I drove north, right over the line into the next county, went to the courthouse. Pudge Phelps is sheriff up there. Pudge and I went across the courthouse square to the market, and I bought us a cup of coffee. I started to tell Pudge the one about the tourist who asks the old-timer if this road goes to Newfane, but Pudge stopped me, said he'd heard that one two hundred and seventy-seven times, and when was I ever going to get some new material? When he and I parted, I got myself a sandwich at the market's deli: ham on rye; I used the department's card for that, too.

By evening, I was on my way back home, on the shortcut that goes through Gilead and Mount Nebo. It was getting dark when I got to Cola's shop. Nobody was there. I drove the truck around back and parked it in the bay. Then I found one of Cola's junkers that ran, and I headed for Mount Nebo.

Pretty far back in the woods, long after the road had turned to dirt, I pulled into a turnout, nudged Cola's beater into the brush, and sat, watching the road in my rear-view. I didn't think anybody would come along, and if they did, they'd take me for a turkey hunter. Nobody came. I ate the sandwich I had bought at Pudge's. I sat. It got good and dark. I sat some more. Did I sleep? It don't seem possible, but I believe maybe I did.

Past midnight, I got started. The turnout where I'd waited was under the north side of Mount Nebo, the easy side. By going straight up and over, I'd get to Cola's camp. There was no road, but on the direct line, it ain't all that far: a couple of miles. I'm still a pretty fair bushwhacker. I had laid out a bearing on the relief map. I had a compass and a flashlight. I also had Wingate's shotgun on a leather sling, bumping and kicking into my lower back with every step I took, like a baby in a backpack, reminding me of what I was about.

I went along pretty well, stopped every now and then to breathe and check the compass. By the time I reached the height of the hill, I was puffing, but the way levelled off, then it started downhill – and not long after that, I saw ahead of me Cola's light.

It was an old kerosene railroad lantern that Cola had rigged on a branch of the big pine where the tree stand was that we had settled on a couple of days before. I found it, blew it out, set it on the ground at the foot of the pine, and played my flashlight up and in amongst the branches to find the ladder steps to the stand's platform. It was easy. Up I went, made myself comfortable, laid the barrel of the Winchester on the railing before me, and looked around.

By the starlight, I could make out the surrounding woods and the opening in them, the little clearing that the tree stand covered. I couldn't see the camp building itself. Maybe an hour to dawn.

A light came on in the distance, hard to tell how far off. A dim light, unmoving. That would be Cola, inside the camp, waiting. A few minutes later, here came more lights, a pair, shifting and bouncing a little. That would be Wingate and the Chairman driving in to the place, down from the camp, where you parked your vehicle. Those lights stopped, and a smaller, single light appeared, moving toward the camp. The Chairman's flashlight. The paired lights backed around and started off the way they had come. Wingate on his way home.

Now you could see the sky above the woods had turned to grey. Somewhere a bird started up with a faint *plink, plank, plunk.*

In a minute, the flashlight left the camp and came slowly toward me where I waited in the tree stand. I could hear Cola

164

and the Chairman moving through the woods, and I could hear them talking, but not to understand. I got myself settled right down, relaxed, with the shotgun braced on the rail pointing out over the opening. I got its stock right up against and a little inboard of my shoulder. I found the tiny brass sight bead at the muzzle. Even in the half-light, I could see it clearly. I took a breath. I cocked the hammer.

Cola and Roark came out of the woods and into the clearing. They were alone: no heavy hitter from upstate. Cola led. The Chairman was right behind him, stamping down the brush as he went.

'Where is he?' Roark asked Cola.

'Right up here,' Cola said.

'God damn it, he must know we're here,' the Chairman said. 'Why doesn't he say anything?'

'Probably gone to sleep,' Cola said. He never looked at me or in my direction. He led the Chairman to within six or seven paces of my position, then sheared off hard right, stepping quickly, leaving the Chairman to come on ahead. The sky was pale now, and the morning fog hung in the clearing and in the woods in white swags and rags, moving, like little kids running here and there, dressed up in old bed sheets for Halloween.

'Where are you going?' the Chairman asked Cola. But he didn't stop. He came right to me. He wasn't looking ahead, he was looking at Cola. I took another breath. I held it. I found the Winchester's trigger with my forefinger. When the Chairman got to the outermost branches of the pine I was in, he stopped, and he looked up. Another two or three steps, and I could have shaken his hand. I think he saw me right at the end, but I'm not sure, because that's when I put the bead on his nose and let go.

***

I climbed down from the stand with my shoulder sore and my ears still ringing. Cola was on one knee beside Stephen Roark. The Chairman was pretty badly busted up around the head and face. Cola held two fingers to the side of his throat. He looked up at me. He waited a few seconds, then he said, 'Done deal,' and got to his feet. Cola was still watching me. He put his hand on my shoulder.

'You all right?' Cola asked me. 'How are you doing? Okay?'

'Better than him,' I said.

'You got that right,' Cola said. He looked at his watch. 'Okay,' he said. 'It's not quite six. How long do you need? Till eight?'

'Make it eight-thirty.'

'Okay,' Cola said. 'Eight-thirty, quarter to nine, I'll call this in. After that, it runs on its own. Right?' He patted my shoulder again.

'Right,' I said. 'Here I go.'

'There was no other way,' Cola said.

'No,' I said.

'We had a situation.' He shrugged.

'We did.'

'See you in church,' Cola said. He turned and started toward the camp, leaving me to get back through the woods.

Where's your Soft Path now, Deputy Gilfeather?

22
Sherlock F. Holmes

One of the firefighters, only a kid, had just finished being sick in the woods. He came back to us, wiping his mouth.

'Sorry,' he said. 'Gee, I'm sorry.'

'Don't worry about it,' Cola told him.

'I thought I was going to be okay,' the firefighter said. 'I don't know. I've never...'

'Forget it,' Cola said. 'Happens to everybody.'

We had a pretty good crowd by now. We had three firefighters, four emergency medical responders with two ambulances, four state police troopers, Cola and me. Yes, a pretty good send-off for the late Chairman. Now we were waiting on the death investigator to come from the state medical examiner's office. Those fellows always take their time; but then, why would they be in a hurry?

The youngest of the four troopers evidently thought he was God's gift to law enforcement. He was pretty sure he knew it all, and he was out to impress the senior trooper on the scene with his brains and with his drive. He wasn't going about it the best way, though, and, in Claude Severance, he might have picked the wrong superior. Claude don't impress easy.

The young trooper had climbed up into the tree stand.

'Somebody's been up here recently,' he called down to the rest of us. 'There's fresh scratches on the boards.'

'Well, of course there's scratches,' Claude told him. 'Of course somebody's been up there. It's turkey season, son. This is a tree stand. What did you expect to find, a Bible? And, look: this guy took a load of number four in the face, close up. What did you think, the shooter was on the Moon? Get your ass back down here.'

Claude and I were interviewing Cola. Mostly it was Claude interviewing. He was taking notes in a little book he kept in his pocket. Dwight Farrabaugh had the same kind of book, I recalled. All the high-up cops have one. I was thinking if this business came off, I'd get a little book for myself. If it didn't, I wouldn't need one, would I?

Cola was telling Claude how his good friend Chairman Steve was an avid turkey hunter. Loved being out there. Steve had been talking about it to Wingate, and Wingate told him about Cola's camp, how they did a lively business up there in turkeys as well as in deer, bear, and so on. The Chairman said that sounded good to him. Wingate asked Cola if he'd be willing to have Steve up to camp sometime, show him the setup. Sure, said Cola, and he told Wingate to tell the Chairman to come on up to camp whenever they were there. The Chairman said he'd like to, but first he just wanted to get the lay of the land, get oriented.

'He wasn't going to hunt, then?' Claude asked Cola.

'Not this time,' Cola said. 'He wanted to scope things out.'

'That was Steve,' I said.

'What you could call an orderly mind,' Cola said. 'Was a military man, you know. He liked to have everything lined up. No surprises.'

'Got a little bit of a surprise this time, though, I guess,' Claude said. 'Didn't he?'

Anyway, Cola went on, he told Steve to come on up to camp first thing this morning. First thing. In turkey hunting, of course, you have to be in the woods, in your spot, well before sunrise when the birds leave their roosts and commence foraging. You have to be waiting for them, and you have to keep perfectly still, because those turkeys are the shyest, sharpest, most alert birds in the woods. Out there with them as you are, before first light, not moving, scarcely breathing, the hardest thing about turkey hunting is staying awake.

'So we left it that Steve would come up this morning,' Cola told Claude. 'I'd be there to show him around. Wingate would drive him up. He was right on time, got here, oh, I guess three-thirty, four o'clock. We had a cup of coffee, and I showed Steve on our map where the stands are. Offered to take him around, but he said no, said he'd rather go by himself. Steve, again: he liked to run his own show. Lucian will tell you the same thing.'

'That's right,' I said.

'What about Wingate?' Claude asked. 'What did he do?'

'Nothing,' Cola said. 'He didn't stay. He would have had to have been carried from the vehicles to camp. He just dropped Steve off, then he went along.'

'Okay,' Claude said.

'So, Steve took his flashlight and went out,' Cola said. 'I stayed here. Had another cup of coffee, got ready to make up a bunch of bacon and eggs.'

'Cola's quite a camp cook,' I said.

'Is that right?' Claude asked.

'No choice,' Cola said. 'I live alone.'

'Okay,' Claude said.

'In an hour or so,' Cola said. 'No sign of Steve. But I didn't think much about it. It was still pitch dark. I thought probably

169

he'd gotten a little turned around and was waiting for sun-up so he could get his bearings and come on in.'

'What I'd do,' I said.

'Okay,' Claude said.

'Then,' Cola said. 'Just before first light, I hear a shot.'

'One shot?' Claude asked him.

'One shot,' Cola said. 'From over this way someplace, but hard to tell just where. Again, I didn't think much about it. We ain't the only hunters up here. Far from it. Woods are full of them, in season. Hell, on the first day of deer hunting, you need a traffic cop in these woods, ain't that right, Lucian?'

'That's right,' I said.

'Okay,' Claude said.

'Another hour, though,' Cola said. 'Now it's broad daylight. Still no sign of Steve. I went outside, I called his name. Nothing. Now I'm a little worried.'

'Okay,' Claude said.

'So, I set out looking for him,' Cola went on. 'Tried the near stand, over there, first. Nobody there. Came on here, found him like you see.'

Cola stopped. He looked down. He shook his head. He swallowed. He choked a little. He shook his head again. 'I just wish I'd made him wear a vest,' he said. 'I never thought of it. Steve wasn't hunting, after all. But if he'd had a vest... Well, I don't know.'

A fat tear ran out of Cola's eye, the hazel one, and down his cheek. He brushed it away. 'I feel like it's my fault,' he said.

'Don't,' Claude said. 'Use your head. What difference would a vest have made? Whoever did this did it practically in the pitch dark. He couldn't see what he was shooting at. He couldn't have seen a vest. That's what happened, you know it is. Fucking sound-shooter, this was. Then, when he sees what he's done, he loses it and takes off. Let it work on him a day or so. He'll come in. Or, if he doesn't, then forget it. We'll never find him, we'll never know what happened here.' He turned to Cola. 'You didn't see anybody when you drove in last night?'

'Sure, I saw people,' Cola said. 'I told you, there's hunters all in through here. I saw a couple of trucks, some guys in a camper. Not right near, but around.'

'Nobody you knew, though?' Claude asked him.

'No,' Cola said.

'So, you found him,' Claude asked. 'What, then?'

'I made sure he was gone, then I came back to camp. No phone there, of course, so I went down to the shop, called Lucian. What was that, about nine?' he asked me.

'Eight-thirty,' I said.

'Eight-thirty, then,' Cola said. 'I called Lucian – the sheriff's office. Here we are.'

'Okay,' Claude said. 'That's it.' He shut his notebook and stowed it away in his pocket.

The four troopers were standing around the Chairman. They kept their backs to the body. It lay face up, with the arms stretched out and one leg doubled under it. It was a mess. Nobody could have told it was the Chairman, except maybe his dentist. The heavy turkey shot had chewed him up that badly. No wonder nobody wanted to look. No wonder the young firefighter lost his breakfast.

Cola and Claude and I went over to the troopers. 'I don't like it,' the bright young trooper was saying. 'If he was hunting and was shot by accident, shot for a turkey, then, if he's hunting, why doesn't he have a gun? Why doesn't he have an orange safety vest? Why doesn't he have a hunting license on him?'

'Because he wasn't hunting, jerkoff,' Claude told him. 'He was scoping the place out. We got the whole story. We got it without you. Believe it or not.'

'I still don't like it,' the trooper said.

'You don't have to like it,' Claude told him. 'What you do have to do is go and get on your radio and see what's keeping the ME. We're done here. Let's roll.'

The young trooper started for the camp and the vehicles. Claude watched him go. He shook his head.

'Sherlock Fucking Holmes, I've got here,' he said.

***

Deputy Gilfeather had missed the action. She'd had a court date in Brattleboro.

'You're lucky you were someplace else,' I told her. 'He was hit right in the face, very close range. Shotgun. I ain't seen anything that bad in a long time. Maybe never.'

'Hunting accident, I guess?' Deputy Gilfeather said.

'Textbook,' I said.

'Nobody saw anybody, any vehicles, anything else?'

'No.'

'No forensics?'

'Not likely, back in the woods, all those people all over the scene.'

'That's it, then?' the deputy asked.

'I guess it is,' I said. 'Staties have pretty much signed off on it.'

'It must happen a fair amount, though, hunting country up here, and all,' the deputy said.

'It does,' I said. 'Usually, it's in deer season. Usually, it's a kid, shoots his hunting buddy, shoots his brother, his dad. Shoots a stranger. He comes forward right off or after a couple of days, turns himself in. Can't stand the guilt.'

'Yes,' the deputy said. 'That's got to be tough on a kid.'

'Very tough, on a kid.'

'So, has anybody come in?'

'No,' I said.

Deputy Gilfeather changed gears. I won't say she was in Clemmie's class for speed at the shift, but she wasn't far off, and she's still young.

'You're back home nights now, right, Sheriff?' she asked me.

'Yes,' I said.

'It must be good to sleep in your own bed.'

'Yes.'

'You recall that time a while back, we talked? That time in your office? Walt's wife thought she'd locked herself out? Walt came in while we were talking?'

'I recall.'

'I've still got that bed,' Deputy Gilfeather said.

'You need to settle down, Deputy,' I told her. 'This is a small town, you know. You don't look out, you'll get a reputation.'

'I already have one, don't I?'

'How do you mean?'

'Ask your mother,' the deputy said.

'Oh,' I said. 'Don't let her bother you.'

'She doesn't bother me,' Deputy Gilfeather said. 'Nothing bothers me. I'm happy. I like it here. I like being a deputy. I like being your deputy. I'm not leaving. I'm staying. I'm going nowhere. I'm stubborn, Sheriff. Don't forget where I came up.'

'Ah,' I said. 'You're talking about The Corps.'

'You've got it.'

'Semper Fi, ain't it?' I asked her.

'Semper Fi, Sheriff,' the deputy said.

***

I let Addison pour me a drink.

'You're drinking?' he said.

'Been a long week,' I said.

'I can see that. Terrible thing.'

'Terrible.'

'I hadn't any particular use for Roark, as you know,' Addison said. 'Nobody did. But to go that way… Terrible. Do you have any leads at all?'

'No,' I said. 'Staties think it had to have been people from away. Hunters from away. They saw what they'd done. They just packed up and took off. Goodbye.'

'You say "they". More than one, you think?'

'No idea.'

'No idea,' Addison said. 'Then there's no real hope we'll ever know.'

'Sometimes that happens. More than a few times.'

'It's hard, though, isn't it? No explanation, no resolution. That's it: no resolution. No end to the story.'

'No end?' I said. 'Sure, there's an end. What I'm always saying: things get sorted out. They get settled. Things come to an end. Leave them alone, they always do.'

'That's been your experience, has it?' Addison asked me.

'You bet,' I said.

'Well, but experience, don't you know, isn't the same as a resolution, is it? We were talking about a resolution. Weren't we?'

'I ain't sure what we were talking about,' I said.

'Me, either. Shall we have another boost?'

'I should be getting home.'

'Well, and there's another thing in this long week,' Addison said. 'A good thing. You're back home, Lucian. Being home is good. Are you sure you won't have another drink?'

'You know?' I said. 'Considering that I'm back home, me and the lass unparalleled, I believe I will.'

23
New Information

Suddenly, Addison and our mother were – what's the word? They were always together. They went to the store together. They went for walks, they went for drives. You saw them at the movies in Brattleboro, holding hands in the dark like high school kids. Inseparable.

'I thought he was going to be watching out for her, you know?' Paul said.

'Making sure she stayed in the corral? This is a lot more than that. I don't get it.' Neither did I. We put in our order for a keeper, and it looked like we'd bought something else. What, exactly?

***

'You don't get it?' Clemmie said. 'So what? You don't have to get it. Neither does Paul – Paul especially. Your mom knew she couldn't go on alone. She wouldn't move in with Paul and The Weeper. She could hardly share your office with you. She didn't want to go into cold storage up at Steep Mountain. Daddy came along and made it so she didn't have to. Everything worked out fine. I don't see Paul's problem.'

***

'Well,' Paul said. 'It doesn't look too good, does it? I mean, it's not like we're talking about the young and the reckless, here, is it? Mom and Addison are supposed to be grownups. God knows they're old enough to be. And here they are living together like a couple of hippies.'

'We don't know how they're living together,' I said.

'We know perfectly well,' Paul said. 'So does everybody else. I'm the school superintendent around here, Lucian. I take that seriously. I don't teach shop. The way I look at it, people trust their kids to me to learn standards for living, standards for conduct. What kind of standards can I hold up for them if my own mother is running around town like some kind of geriatric camp follower?'

'Oh, come on.'

'I'm sorry,' Paul said. 'That's how I see it.'

***

'What a jerk,' Clemmie said. 'Tell him to go take a jump.'

'You tell him,' I said.

'I'll be glad to,' Clemmie said.

She will, too.

***

'*Geriatric camp follower*,' Addison laughed. 'Paul said that? Your brother, Paul?'

'That's what he said.'

'Geriatric camp follower is pretty good,' Addison said. 'I didn't think Paul had that kind of wit.'

'Paul can be real witty,' I said.

'Hah,' Addison said. 'He's not the only one. Look, Lucian, we're not going to talk about your mother and me. Lorraine and I have known each other all our lives. I knew Brad. Hell, if it hadn't been for a heart murmur, I might have *been* Brad. In a manner of speaking.'

'Because of the war, you mean.'

'That's right,' Addison said. 'I missed it. I wasn't draftable: funny ticker. The war wouldn't have me, don't you know. So Brad, at twenty-one or -two, goes out and never comes back, and here I sit, a lifetime later, old and fat and happy. That's how war works, isn't it? There's nothing for it. Now comes your old widowed mother. She needs a place to go. I have a place. I'm an old friend. What am I going to tell her, no?'

'You say you knew my father,' I said. 'Paul says you knew him well. You two were close, Paul says. Right?'

Addison looked at me and started to answer, then he stopped. He shook his head.

'I said I knew Brad,' Addison said. 'I didn't say I knew him well.'

***

'Paul's a good man,' our mother said. 'He's a good superintendent. He takes himself too seriously. I blame that Wendy.'

'Wendy can be a little serious,' I said.

'A little? She's a one-man funeral,' Mom said.

'You could say that.'

'Now, you take The Infanta,' Mom went on. 'Your Clementine and I haven't always gotten on the best, but we understand each other. She's got a good heart. You're lucky to have her. You know that, right?'

'Sure,' I said. 'Sure, I do. I'm back at home, now, you know. We're together again.'

'He told me.'

'He?'

'Lawyer Jessup – Addison,' Mom said. 'Come to that, I suppose I could move on in with you and The Infanta now, couldn't I?'

'Are you asking?'

'No, sir,' our mother said. 'I am situated.'

'I'm glad to hear it,' I said.

'I'm fine,' Mom said. 'It's you. And don't give me *sure*. You know what I'm saying. I'm saying, don't blow it.'

'What are you talking about?'

'What do you think I'm talking about? Do I not hear what everybody says about you two? Your so-called marriage?'

'Careful. You're starting to sound like Paul. Like Wendy.'

'God forbid. But, remember this is a small town.'

'That's the same thing I told my deputy,' I said.

'You and that deputy. That's another thing.'

'No, it ain't,' I said. 'If you think there's anything to know about me and Deputy Gilfeather, you're nutser than any of us thought.'

'Suppose I believe you,' our mother said. 'That still leaves you and the Clemmie. Don't screw that up.'

'It's pretty screwed up already, ask me,' I said.

'No,' our mother said. 'It's the way you and she work things out. It doesn't matter *how* you work them out, it matters *that* you do. Everybody's different. You and the Infanta have something special.'

'That's for damn sure,' I said.

***

'Nobody told you?' Cola asked me. 'About that fellow – that friend of the late Mr. Roark?'

'Not a friend, exactly, was he?' Wingate said.

'Nobody told you about him?' Homer asked me.

'Sutton,' Cola said. 'Vinnie Sutton. Investigator from – I don't know where.'

'State's attorney's office,' Homer said. 'Some such.'

'I know who you mean,' I said. 'What about him?'

'He was here,' Cola said. 'You didn't hear about that?'

I shook my head.

'Shows up at the shop one day last week,' Cola said. Funny-looking, fat little fellow, not what you'd think he'd be. Little pot belly on him. Bow tie. Wore a porkpie hat. Says he's looking into the death of Stephen Roark, understands I had information. I told him that's right, told him about Roark coming up to camp, wants to have a look at the turkey action, goes out to the tree stands on his own. Told him about how I heard a shot, went and found him. Told him the whole thing.'

''Course, you did,' Homer said. 'No problem.'

'Then he asks me about Homer,' Cola went on. 'Said he had a witness who'd put Homer at one of the assault-and-battery cases in the valley. Did I have any light to shed on that? I told him if he had business with Homer, then he should take it up with Homer, not me.'

'I haven't heard from him,' Homer told me. 'I feel neglected, kind of, you know?'

'Then,' Cola said, 'Sutton wants to go up, look over camp.'

'Again, no problem,' Homer said.

'So, I drive him up there,' Cola went on. 'Sutton wants me to show him where I found Roark. I show him. Then he says I'm to go on back to camp, wait there, leave him to do his job. I go. I don't think much about it. Everything's covered, ain't it? Then, not ten minutes later, here comes Sutton, and he's got our lantern.'

'What lantern?' I asked him.

'You know,' Cola said. 'The old railroad lantern I lit and hung out to mark the stand tree for you when you had to bushwhack up there in the dark. That lantern.'

'That lantern,' I said. 'I thought you'd taken it, I guess.'

'I thought you had,' Cola said.

'Now Sutton's found it,' Cola said. 'He asked me if that's my lantern.'

'What did you tell him?' I asked.

'I told him I never saw that lantern before in my life,' Cola said. 'That lantern was a new lantern to me, I told him.'

'And...?' I said.

'He bought it,' Homer said.

'Handed me the lantern,' Cola said. 'Told me, "Well, I guess it's yours now." Then he said, "Want to get started? I've got a lunch in White River."'

'That was it?' I asked.

'Almost,' Wingate said. 'Tell him what he said, the state's attorney's fellow.'

'We were driving back down here,' Cola said. 'I asked him how the Roark investigation was going.'

'He asked, what investigation?' Wingate said.

'"What investigation?" Sutton asked me,' Cola said. 'Then he said the only reason to try to find out who shot Roark, or why, would be to know where to send the medal.'

'Man was an asshole, he said,' Cola added.

'Meaning Roark,' Homer said. ''Course,' he went on, 'Cola didn't like to hear that, having a high opinion of Chairman Steve like he did. Practically brothers, weren't they, Cola and Roark?'

'The way Lucian said Cola took on when they found Roark at the stand?' Wingate said. 'Like somebody'd run over his dog. Bawled like a baby, didn't he, Lucian?'

'Okay, okay,' Cola said.

'Good old Vinnie,' Wingate said.

'Good old Vinnie, is right,' Cola said. 'That fucking lantern, you know? When I saw him with it, I thought... I don't know what I thought.'

'Thought you were going to shit your britches, I'll bet, is what you thought, ain't it?' Homer asked him.

'I won't deny it,' Cola said. 'But that's another thing: that lantern. Where did that lantern come from, in the first place? I don't recall.'

'I do,' Wingate said. 'That was one of Brad's lanterns.'

'Brad's?' Cola asked.

'That's right,' Wingate said. 'Before your time. Brad had three or four of those lanterns – this is, oh, years ago. That must be the last of them. It seems like he'd had a job on the railroad or something, one summer, got them there. He brought them up to camp, used them for deer. He and Addison.'

'And Lorrie,' Homer said. 'Don't forget Lorrie. Brad and Addison went up there a good deal. Sometimes Lorrie went along. She hunted, too. They used Brad's lanterns for shining deer.'

'Lorrie, my mother?' I asked Homer.

'Shining something, anyway,' Homer said.

'What's that mean?' Cola asked him. '"Shining something?"'

'Well,' Homer said. 'Just the way Brad and Addison were. Remember Addley and Braddison? They were close.'

'No,' I said. 'Addison didn't know my dad that well, he told me.'

'Well, he would, though, wouldn't he?' Homer said. 'Tell you that.'

'He would?' I asked.

'Way things turned out,' Homer said.

'What things?' I asked. 'Turned out how?'

'Not know Brad?' Homer went on. 'Brad and Addison were thick as thieves People used to call them Addley and Braddison? And then, with Lorrie? But Lorrie always liked Brad best.'

'My mother?' I asked Homer.

'Or maybe she didn't,' Homer said.

'My mother?'

'She married him,' Cola said.

'But then he went to the war, Brad did,' Homer said. 'Addison didn't. What did he do? I guess he went to college and so on.'

'But he was around?' Cola asked.

'Oh, I'd say so,' Homer said. 'Addison was around. Lorrie was around. They were both around. Brad was the one wasn't around. It was Addison and Lorrie.'

'My mother?' I asked.

'You bet,' Homer said. 'So, what Addison tells you? It all ain't necessarily so.'

'It ain't?' I asked.

'Fellows?' Wingate said.

'So maybe Lorrie didn't like Brad best, after all,' Homer said. 'I mean, like I said, when you look at the way things turned out.'

'Things?' I asked.

'What things?' Cola asked.

'Fellows?' Wingate said again.

'What?' Homer asked him.

'Shut up, now, why don't you?' Wingate said. He was talking to Homer and Cola, but he was looking at me.

'Oh,' Homer said. 'Oops.'

'Oops,' Cola said.

'Wait a minute,' I said.

***

'Wait a minute,' Clemmie said.

'That's what I said.'

'Wait a minute. What are you telling me?'

'You know what.'

'You're telling me that all those nightgowns your mother brought with her to Daddy's: they weren't to make her look

182

pretty for your father; they were to make her look pretty for *my* father. That's what you're telling me. Right?'

'I am telling you that,' I said. 'I'm telling you more. I'm telling you, your father and my father? Same fellow.'

'That can't be,' Clemmie said. 'That means...'

'That's what it means,' I said.

'I have to think about this,' Clemmie said. 'This is new information.'

'It sure is,' I said. 'Ain't it, Sis.'

'My Lord,' Clemmie said.

'So,' I went on, 'this new information? I know you have to think about it, but could you tell me whether you want to think about it here or go someplace else to think about it? Reason I ask? It's new information for me, too, and I've had about enough new information for awhile.'

'You have?' Clemmie asked me.

'I have,' I said. 'And I ain't going back to the couch.'

'I wonder if Daddy knows,' Clemmie said.

'So do I,' I said.

Envoi

Wingate lit a cigar and tossed the match off the porch and onto the grass. He sat back in his chair.

'You heard about Cola, I guess,' he said.

'I heard he had the camp up for sale,' I said. 'I don't suppose he'll have an easy time finding a buyer.'

'He's already found one,' Wingate said.

'He has? Who?'

'Some outfit in Brattleboro. They want to turn the place into a nature centre.'

'What kind of a nature centre?'

'I don't know. How many kinds are there? A nature centre. They've been after Cola for years to sell it to them, he says. They say there's all kinds of rare plants and animals up there. There's stuff up there you don't see nowhere else.'

'You got that right,' I said.

'They want to make it into a camp.'

'It's already a camp.'

'No,' Wingate said, 'not a hunting camp, a camp with campers. Kids. They'll go out in the woods, study the animals, the wildlife, study the trees. The birds. A nature centre.'

'Surprises me Cola would do that,' I said. 'Sell camp up, I mean. His grandfather had that place.'

'His great-grandfather had it,' Wingate said. 'Surprised me, too. Homer says it's because Cola was pretty spooked by the whole thing with Mr. Roark, there. That situation.'

'Spooked?'

'What Homer said.'

'Why's Cola spooked?' I asked Wingate. 'He's not the one that did it. I am.'

'We all are,' Wingate said. 'That's how it works, ain't it? How it used to work. Now, with no more camp, it won't work that way any more.'

'No,' I said. 'It won't.'

Wingate smoked his cigar. After a minute, he said, 'You know, people have funny ideas about little places like we've got up here. You know that? They think nothing ever goes wrong or gets out of whack in them. And then, when things do, when there's situations, you know? People think they take care of themselves.'

'Well, nine times out of ten, that's so,' I said.

'Well,' Wingate said, 'but, no, it ain't. Situations don't take care of themselves by magic. They take care of themselves because of Cola's camp, as you might say, because of people like the people at camp, people like us, who will do what has to be done and, when it's done, who can carry the weight of it. People like that are getting scarce. And now, with no more camp? I don't know.'

'You're saying Cola can't carry the weight any more?' I asked.

'He don't think he can, it looks like,' Wingate said. 'All that Roark thing, and then that fellow from upstate. That was pretty close. That fellow had his own business going, I guess, but if he hadn't, if he'd gone right straight ahead – well, it's good he didn't.'

'It sure is,' I said.

'I can see it, I guess,' Wingate said. 'How it would get to Cola, a little bit. That Roark thing went right up to the wall,

185

didn't it? That was pretty rough. That wasn't scorching some dumb kid's ass to show him the path of righteousness. Was it?'

I smiled at that. 'No,' I said.

'So,' Wingate said, 'that's on Cola's mind, it looks like. Why he's selling camp. Too bad.'

'Maybe. But it is his to sell.'

'So it is. But I wish he wouldn't. Cola should lighten up, you ask me. Tell you what it is? The whole thing? It's just bad news and good news, like everything else, ain't it?'

'How do you mean?'

'Well,' Wingate said. 'Bad news is, we did an evil thing. An evil thing. No two ways about it. We did murder. Good news is, we got away with it. And we took care of the situation.'

The ash fell from the end of Wingate's cigar and landed on his chest and stomach.

'Look at that,' Wingate said. 'Dribbled on my pinafore.' He brushed the spilled ash away with his hand.

'Speaking of good news,' Wingate said. 'I hear you're off the department's couch. You're back in the marriage bed again, I hear.'

'That's right,' I said.

'What's it like?' Wingate asked me.

'What's what like?'

'Well,' Wingate said. 'That. Being married.'

'I've been married some years,' I said.

'But, married like now you know you are.'

'I don't know,' I said. 'It's different, and it ain't. Ask Clemmie.'

'I don't think so,' Wingate said. 'Anyway, good on you.'

'Thanks,' I said. 'You're a little out of date, though.'

'I'm always out of date,' Wingate said. 'How now, in particular?'

'I've been back home for three–four weeks,' I told him.

'That long?' Wingate said. 'I hadn't heard. See, what it is, nobody tells me nothing.'

Preview

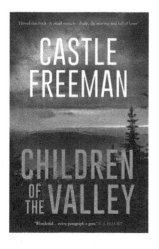

Sheriff Lucian Wing goes to the aid of a pair of young runaways, Duncan and Pamela, who have fled to his backwoods county jurisdiction in Vermont. The girl's powerful New York stepfather has set a smoothly menacing lawyer and well-armed thugs on their trail.

At the same time Wing must deal with his wayward wife's chronic infidelity; the snobbery of Pamela's cosmopolitan mother; the dubious assistance of a demented World War Two enthusiast – and even the climactic, chaotic onset of a prodigious specimen of the local wildlife.

Amidst it all, can Wing bring Duncan and Pamela to safety?

Also Available

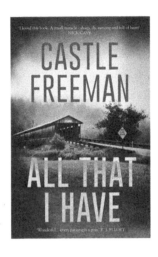

Lucian Wing is an experienced, practical man who enforces the law in his corner of Vermont with a steady hand and a generous tolerance. But when local tearaway Sean 'Superboy' Duke starts to get tangled up with a group of major league Russian criminals, things start to go awry in the sheriff's small, protected domain.

With an ambitious and aggressive deputy snapping at his heels and a domestic crisis of his own to confront, Wing must call on all the personal resources he has cultivated during his working life: patience, tact, and – especially – humour.

Can Wing's low-key approach to law enforcement prevail?

About Castle Freeman's Novels

'Practically all the writing I have done – fiction, essays, history, journalism, and more – has been in one way or another about rural northern New England, in particular the State of Vermont, and the lives of its inhabitants, a source of unique and undiminishing interest, at least to me.'

The Lucian Wing novels –

All That I Have

Old Number Five

Children of the Valley

Other –

Go With Me

The Devil in the Valley

About the Author

Castle Freeman was born in 1944 in San Antonio, Texas. He was brought up on the South Side of Chicago, and later went to college in New York. In 1972, he moved with his wife to the southeastern corner of Vermont, where they have remained since.

He is an award-winning author not only of fiction, but also of personal essays, reporting, op-ed matter, history and natural history. He has been a regular contributor to several periodicals, including *The Old Farmer's Almanac* (1982–2011).

Note from the Publisher

To receive background material and updates on new releases by Castle Freeman, sign up at farragobooks.com/castlefreeman-signup